Silent Siren

A HOLLYWOODLAND MYSTERY

A. G. Macdonald

MACDONALD

Praise for Cinderella: Dead at 25!

"First and foremost, don't be fooled: This is not simply a fairy tale retelling."

"I felt transported in time, watching this story unfold in black and white as I read with anticipation of what will happen next."

"I have read a lot of books, but I've not read a book like this."

the Hollywood Scoop

Vol 16, Issue No 72   News for today   Stories forom around the world   News that matters, Now!   25c

SILENT SIREN SHUNS STAR

ACTRESS CAROLINE LAKE EXPOSED AS A FRAUD IN NEW SHOCK CLAIMS

Caroline Lake has stolen the voice of young Bailey

The actress met the singer at her local gin joint: The Neptune Lounge

ma in the award winning picture *Tears of Hope*. But now the actress has been exposed after it was release of her latest film, a film adaptation of the hit stage musical *Bloomer Girl*. But Miss Lake Stole the the voice of a lounge singer named Billie Bailey. Miss Bailey seemed to befriend the actress; a friendship that opportunistic Lake was more than happy to exploit. She used the young singer, then took credit for her work (continued on page 6)

Caroline Caught in Callous Coup

Polly Whittingham

Hollywood is in shock today as yet another crime has taken plaace in this magical city of ours. Only this time, the only crime that has been committed, it is the one against our ears. Miss Lake, most notablly known for her role as Vel-

(continued on page 6)

Chapter 1

April 1946

Manuel Martinez's eyes bulged out his skull like a character from a Betty Boop cartoon. His head tilted to the left, but he stared forward, his rust-brown irises drilling into Rex's soul. A chilly breeze whistled down the grimy alleyway, carrying the stink of rotting garbage. The private detective stared at the corpse, unable to look away, like a traffic accident he was too far away to stop. He removed his Homburg hat and held it to his chest.

Blood trickled under the corpse's grey pants, splitting rivulets down the cracked pavement that glistened under the pink neon of some seedy Skid Row dive bar just beyond the corner of the short alley. A tingle settled over Rex as the hairs on the back of his neck stood on end.

Someone was watching.

Behind him, in a second-floor window, a thin curtain flicked open. A bug-eyed youth stared before he closed the drapes and peeked through again. Paranoia glistened in the kid's eyes from the darkened room, probably his first shot at reefer. But the boy's nervous energy extended beyond the side effects of loco weed. The kid knew something.

Rex stepped away from the body and inspected the brick wall. Deep gouges ran through the red bricks, traveling to the garage below the kid's window. Mr. Martinez had been waiting for Rex because he couldn't make it to his office on the Sunset Strip. The doped-out kid must've decided to get high and take his father's car out for a drive. He plowed down Mr. Martinez, parked his car in the garage, and now hid in his bedroom, waiting for the police to haul him to jail. And judging the sirens wailing in the distance, they weren't far off.

A weight pressed on Rex's chest as he turned back to face the body. If it weren't for Rex, the man wouldn't be in the alley in the first place. The screeching of tires pulled Rex from his thoughts as a black and white Ford patrol car pulled up across the alleyway, sirens howling. A silhouette stepped from the vehicle towards him in the flashing red light that saturated the alleyway.

"Step away from the body, Sir," said the man as he withdrew his pistol.

Rex held his hands in the air.

"I didn't have anything to do with this, officer," said Rex.

"Get on the ground."

"But—"

"On the ground! Now!" the policeman ordered.

Rex crouched down and winced as his arthritic knees screamed in agony. He was only at a gentle bend and wasn't sure if his joints would snap before he made it to the blood-stained pavement, but he pushed on with a grimace.

"Wait a minute," said the policeman. "Horne?"

Rex stood upright as the officer's silhouette disappeared, and a young man in a navy blue pinstripe suit snapped into focus, a crisp pork pie hat tilted over his eyes.

"Sorry," said Rex, "but do I know you?"

The man pulled a pack of Camels from his pocket, drew one out, and held it between his lips.

"Horne, you old son of a gun." He chuckled as he sparked up. "You always did have an odd sense of humor."

Rex chuckled along with the deranged policeman; probably best not to anger a lunatic with a gun. The man dragged his cigarette and blew peppery smoke across the alley like a poorly tuned dump truck. He tilted his hat up in the dispersing smoke. His baby blue eyes sparkled as the young kid smirked at him.

"Chaz," he said. "Chaz Benson. I can't believe you would forget me like that. I thought what we went through bonded us for life. You know, a band of brothers and all that."

Rex shook his head. "I remember you, Chaz."

Private Charles Benson wasn't easy to forget. Rex's senior officer lumped the brat into the 407th because his father was some head honcho at command—and Benson let everybody know. The second things weren't up to the kid's satisfaction, or he missed out on some plum assignment, then it was straight to daddy. The number of times Rex's superiors called on him to check in on the little jackanape sent a lightning bolt of pain through his head even now. Still, he managed to keep the kid in line; but the barracks were a couple of years and a million miles away.

Not that things had changed too much for Benson. Daddy must have pulled a few strings to get the kid promoted to detective at the LAPD, judging by the expensive suit. But the costume didn't do him any favors. The weedy little boy with sandy blonde hair and blue eyes looked like a kid playing dress-up in his father's work clothes.

"How long has it been?" asked Benson. "I haven't seen you since—"

"Brittany," muttered Rex. "Still hasn't been long enough."

Benson chuckled and slapped him on the shoulder.

"This is crazy, huh?" said Chaz. "You were once my superior officer, and now I'm here with Vice. It's almost like I'm your boss. It's a gas, huh?"

"A scream." Rex arched an eyebrow.

"Although you kinda landed on your feet after the war. I saw you solved that big Cinderella case, and now you're seeing that actress Virginia Lancaster. She's a bit long in the tooth for me; a bit more your speed. Good for you, Horne."

Rex balled his fist. The kid's taut smirk made the private detective genuinely contemplate whether it was worth breaking his vow and going three rounds in the ring with the kid, just to teach him a lesson. Rex drew a deep breath. Every muscle tensed before he let go, and the anger flowed out his fingertips like water through a faucet.

"So, how did you know the stiff?" asked Benson.

"He was a client." Rex turned back to Mr. Martinez. "Asked me to find his brother for him."

"Did you?" asked Benson.

Murmurs echoed around the corner, followed by a man's voice shouting, "There he is!"

A gaggle of reporters and photographers tumbled down the street, bulbs blinking, yelling over one another. Benson shot Rex a wince before turning to the crowd and unleashing an exaggerated groan.

"Alright." He put his hands up in the air, flashing a smile for the cameras. "I've got your story right here."

But the reporters shoved past him and flashed their camera bulbs in Rex's eyes with a dull crack. He held a hand over his eyes, unable to see the men's faces.

"Mr. Horne," one man shouted through the blinding lights. "What're you doing here. I thought you only took on the high-profile cases these days. Or does this have something to do with a celebrity? Who killed this man? Lana Turner? James Stewart?"

"Maybe it was Ginger Rogers?" shouted another voice.

The group all burst into laughter.

"Maybe it was Virginia Lancaster!" shouted a different voice. "You covering this up for the little lady, Horne? Is that why you're slumming it out here on Skid Row?"

Rex clenched his jaw. If he didn't flip his wig over Benson, then he wasn't going to waste his breath on the pissant reporter. But Benson drew his pistol and held it to the man's temple.

"Show some respect," he said. The photos stopped. The men went deathly quiet. "This man is a war hero, and you stroll in here and accuse him of murder. Who do you think you are?"

The man gulped as his skin turned the color of curdled cream. "It was only a joke, sir."

Benson cocked his gun. "It doesn't seem so funny anymore, does it?"

Rex stepped between him and the reporter. "Charles, that's enough."

"Keep your skirt on, Horne," Benson laughed. "I'm not gonna do anything crazy. I'm here to protect and serve, make sure everybody's safe. Maybe I'll check this fat head's car. It'd be a shame if I found a sizeable stash of T.N.T. in it."

"T.N.T.?" the reporter's voice trembled.

"Heroin." The man lowered his voice. "Terrible stuff it is, ruins lives, you know. What do you think would happen if your wife found out you were into that junk?"

"Sorry," said the reporter. "I just—"

"You just what?"

Benson stowed his gun and moved in a few inches from the man's waxy face, shimmering under the neon light as he backed against the brick wall. The performance was nothing more than a kid playing cops and robbers. The kid had seen *This Gun for Hire* one too many times and no doubt pictured himself as Robert Preston as he curled a limp-wristed grasp around his Colt revolver like it was a water pistol; not the official grip Rex taught him in the service. Despite the pathetic display, the reporter reduced his lips to a thin line as he offered a tight nod. Benson tilted his head side to side, inspecting the man's twitching face. Then a spasmodic laugh escaped the vice detective's lips.

"That's right. See, now you're starting to get the hang of how things work around here. So why don't you apologize to Mr. Horne, the war hero, and then you can hurry back home to Mommy."

"Yes, officer," the man's voice trembled as he nodded to the brat half his age.

The reporters scampered away like rats down the stinking alley. Benson turned to him and laughed.

"So did you find the kid's brother?" asked Benson, as though a passing tourist had interrupted their conversation.

"What?" asked Rex, still picturing the reporter with a gun to his head. "Oh, Mr. Martinez. No, I thought I had for a moment, but then the trail went cold."

"You should join the LAPD because heaps of our guys did it after the war. You won't make Vice as I did right away, but if you work hard, you never know."

Rex fought the urge to roll his eyes. It was painfully clear that merit had nothing to do with the selection criteria, but he smiled as he shook his head.

"Yeah, I don't think it's for me." Rex shrugged.

"Don't dismiss it right away," said Benson. "We also consult with private dicks all around the city. You should think about it. We have files and resources that the public can't access."

Benson reached into his pocket and pulled out a crisp business card. Rex clenched his jaw as he snatched it and stuffed it into his trench coat pocket. It was like making a deal with Mephistopheles. He was waiting for the other shoe to drop and the gun-wielding maniac to reveal his true motives. If what Rex had just witnessed was Los Angeles' finest, then he had no interest in joining the man's freakshow of corruption and measuring gun calibers.

"Think about it, Horne. It'll be like the good old days."

Rex sniggered. "And by good old days, you mean *the war*?"

"You're making this more complicated than it needs to be," said Benson. "One thing I learned in Vice is that the answer to these things is often simple. People just overcomplicate things. Take this kid, for example, Mr. Hernandez. He probably owed some drug dealer money, and this was payback to send a message to all the other low lives on Skid Row who try to mess with them."

Rex glanced up at the open second-floor window, which swished against the cool breeze. Rex pictured the kid sitting behind the drapes, chewing his nails, scanning the room with his bug eyes. The kid was probably in his own hell after what had happened, especially after he sobered in the morning. Besides, Rex couldn't turn the kid into Benson. The arrogant Vice cop had pulled a gun on a reporter for making statements about Rex, which he suspected were less out of defending his honor and more to do with proving that he was a grown-up with a gun.

"Thanks for the offer, but I'm happy where I am now."

"Just think about it," said Benson. "There are a lot of people out there you could help. Hell, you might've been able to save this kid."

"We can't save everyone," Rex glanced to the second-floor window. "Some people just get caught up in the wrong crowd, and things like this happen. There's nothing we could do about it."

"It's always the simplest answer." Benson shrugged.

"You're right." Rex nodded. "A drug deal gone wrong."

Chapter 2

"Mr. H, you got this all wrong."

Suzie Ford sprang to her feet from behind the redwood desk in the foyer of Horne Investigations. Sunlight filtered through the frosted glass panels that partitioned his office, bouncing off her golden ringlets, shining against the cream-colored walls. The receptionist repainted them a month ago and plastered them with framed newspaper clippings of the Cinderella case. It seemed a little arrogant, but Suzie insisted it looked more legitimate. His girl Friday trotted over, her high heels clacking against the polished floorboards.

"My mistake," said Rex. "For a second there, I thought you were asking to leave work early."

"No." Suzie shook her head, thrashing the word with her thick Jersey accent. "Well, I mean, I am, but there is a perfect reason for it."

"And what's that?" Rex headed for his office door.

"It's big news, Mr. H."

The receptionist's Chantilly perfume filled the room with a subtle mixture of orange and lemon as the girl trembled like a bottle rocket about to explode. Rex sighed, then nodded for her to unleash her big news. There was little chance it would be something interesting; usually Suzie gossiped which celebrities had been found with hookers, and which were suspected homosexuals. The detective solved one celebrity case, and all of a sudden everybody expected him to care about the skeletons that lurked beneath the squeaky clean surfaces. Suzie's *big news* was probably some overpriced new restaurant featured in The Hollywood Scoop that proclaimed Humphrey Bogart or Lauren Bacall dined there every night. But Rex gave her a nod to go ahead. The sooner it started, the sooner it finished.

"I met a doctor," she squeaked. "A real-life doctor. I thought it only happened in the movies."

"Most doctor's do have wives," Rex mumbled.

"Come on, Mr. H. Don't be a grump."

Suzie pouted her lips and clapped her hands together in prayer, clicking her acrylic fingernails together. She opened her eyes wide and flicked a glance at him every few seconds.

"You know, every time you do this lost little puppy routine, it loses some of its sting," Rex muttered.

The whole thing was so calculated, but the worst part was it still worked. Rex never had a child, but he imagined she would be like Suzie, so perhaps it was for the best he wasn't a father.

Rex shifted past the girl, grabbed the brass doorknob, and opened his office door. She stepped out of his way and rummaged around the coffee corner by the entrance. The detective hobbled across the mid-sized office to his new carved mahogany desk, Suzie returned to the doorway with a coffee in a white diner mug.

"You gotta understand, Mr. H," she said as she raced the concave cup over and skilfully placed it on the desk without spilling a drop.

"Chances like this don't grow on trees. This could be the one, the love of my life, like that movie *The Doctor Takes a Wife*."

"Don't they hate each other at the start of that film?"

"Well, now you're just splitting hairs, Mr. H," Suzie's voice went up. "Look, this is important to me, and I'd hate to call my mother and tell her that you kept me back and missed out on my chance to go on a date with a doctor. Maybe you could make the call for me."

She may as well have been Rex's daughter, playing him off against her mother like that. Still, he was powerless against her act. Besides, he only ever locked horns with Mrs. Ford once before, after he had to let Suzie go in the dark days before the Cinderella case. The woman nearly chewed his ear off. It didn't matter how many times he told her he had no money. The woman screamed at him with sob stories about dead relatives and threats that her second cousin on her mother's side was a lawyer. She bleated on about taking him for everything he had, which if she had bothered to listen, she would've known was nothing.

An icy shiver traveled down his spine. The banshee was relentless, and he had too much work to do to spend an hour on the phone with the insufferable broad, and judging by the cheeky smirk on his receptionist's face, she knew it too.

"Fine." Rex took a sip of his silky black coffee. "You're just lucky you make a good cup of Joe."

Oh, you're an Angel, Mr. H," said Suzie before she flung her arms around Rex and planted a kiss on his cheek. "You're gonna love him. He's kind and thoughtful, the kind of guy that still holds a door open for a lady. They're getting harder to find, you know."

"Where is this bum taking you? Somewhere nice, I hope. You don't want a doctor who's a cheapskate."

"He's not taking me anywhere nice." A proud grin smeared across Suzie's face. "He's a doctor. He probably has to beat the girls off with a stick, and what do they all want from him?"

"It's Hollywood, so I'm guessing money."

"Exactly," Suzie shouted, folding her arms. "Well, I'm going to be different. I'm going to show him that money isn't the most important thing. So I insisted I decide where we go. A good old-fashioned date on the cheap, like when we were kids."

"You're twenty-three, Suzie," Rex chuckled. "When you get as old as I am, that's *still* a kid."

"So, I told him," Suzie plowed through Rex's comment and continued. "I said, 'David, we're going out to Pink's over on North Le Brea for hot dogs, then we're going to Hunley's Theater on Hollywood Boulevard to see *Bloomer Girl.*"

"Don't you think that title seems a little—"

Rex arched an eyebrow at his receptionist. It sounded like the kind of blue movie that would draw in the type of crowds that Vice cops like Benson rounded up daily. His pseudo fatherly instincts kicked in. Despite her ditsy persona, Suzie was a bright girl who knew how to take care of herself, and he needed to trust that. Suzie shot him a look, then burst into cackles of laughter.

"You think I'm going to take David on a first date to see some illegal humping movie," she giggled. "You need to get your mind out of the gutter, Mr. H."

"Well, with a title like *Bloomer Girl*—"

"It's a musical," she rolled her eyes.

"That's almost as bad. You can't take a man on a first date to see a musical."

Suzie giggle. "What're you talking about?"

"Trust me. It's a terrible idea."

Suzie threw her hands on her hips. "What've you got against musicals?"

"The whole thing doesn't make a lick of sense, with everyone dancing around to spontaneous choreography that clearly took weeks to put together, while they all sing songs nobody's ever heard and yet they all know the words. It's like living inside the head of a lunatic."

"Well, not everybody is as miserable as you, Mr. H," said Suzie. "Some of us choose to enjoy ourselves when we go out. Besides, perhaps you just haven't given any of these movies a chance."

Rex folded his arms and leaned back in his swivel chair. "Suzie, I go to see a couple of movies a week. I've seen plenty: *Meet Me in St. Louis*, *The Pirate*, *Babes on Broadway*."

"Perhaps you got a problem with Judy Garland." Suzie folded her arms, mirroring the private detective.

"There's nothing wrong with the songs. A couple of them are even a little catchy. It's the crazy logic of the world that really drives me around the bend."

"It's make-believe. You're overthinking it." Suzie paused and glanced at her desk behind the glass partition. "Although it's funny you should mention that, because this movie is copping a lot of guff from the press."

Without another word, Suzie disappeared for a few seconds. Her blurry silhouette clattered about her desk behind the frosted windows. She trotted back into the office up to his desk and tossed

the newspaper at him, chewing her lip, that bottle rocket look in
her eye. The six-inch headline swelled to filled a third of the front
page.

SILENT SIREN SHUNS STAR.

"It's a scandal," said Suzie. "Caroline Lake, you remember her
from *Tears of Hope* a couple of years back? Well, she decided to
break into the musicals. Everybody said she was so good, and they
thought she might even get all sorts of awards for it. She was that
good. But then it turns out she wasn't even singing in the picture."

"So you could say it was all a lie."

"Very funny, Mr. Man," she sniggered. "No, this broad could sing
about as well as a cat taking a bath, and now The Hollywood Scoop
found out she used some poor colored girl's voice and paid her off
with a pittance, didn't even give her credit."

"Just proves what I said before, doesn't it?" Rex shrugged. "It's all
a lie. Look, I know none of the movies are real, but we're expected
to believe that this woman talks in one voice and sings in another."

"Don't ruin it now," said Suzie. "You don't want to put me in a
bad mood and have to tell my mother why my date when so badly."

Rex rifled through some documents on his table but never lifted
his head as he said, "No, we definitely don't want that."

Suzie left, but stopped in the doorway for a moment, then
turned back. "There was one other thing, you had a phone call."

"I can see why that nearly slipped your mind after the big
breakdown of that musical I didn't want to see."

"Look at you, cracking jokes left and right today. You thinking
of quitting being a private dick and becoming a funny man?" Suzie

shot him a side-eye. "A detective called from the LAPD He said to call him back about his offer. He said you would know all about it."

"Yeah," said Rex as he went through the documents on his desk.

"Well? Would you like to call him back?"

Rex finally lifted his head from the paperwork. "About as much as I would like to call your mother."

Rex scoured the Yellow Pages for Mr. Martinez's brother Hector. He called every H. Martinez in California, but none claimed to know the deceased. Rex rubbed his temples and closed his eyes with a long sigh. Next thing, he woke to a knocking sound with his nose wedged in the Yellow Pages, drooling all the way to the Martingales. He glanced at his gold watch. It was four o'clock in the afternoon.

"Are you alright?" asked Suzie, standing in the doorway in a fitted grey coat with matching hat, her handbag on her arm.

"Fine," said Rex, managing his best attempt at a smile.

"Well, I'm heading off now. Wish me luck."

"Goodnight, Suzie." said Rex.

The receptionist's blue eyes dropped to the floor as she turned to leave. Rex cleared his throat and she spun back to face the detective.

"Make sure that bum pays for those hotdogs." Rex kept his eyes on his work. "Sweet kid like you deserves it."

"Thanks." She smiled. "You should get home early too. You've got a little lady at home you don't want to disappoint."

Chapter 3

Virginia's laughter permeated the air like the first crack of light breaking over the horizon. Her angelic giggle floated over the cavernous living room and echoed around the periwinkle wallpaper on the second-floor landing. One tiny twinkle in a dark string of disappointments. A million loose ends niggled at the back of Rex's brain as he sat on the white sofa. He rested his elbows on his shins, leaned forward, and ran a hand through his hair. Manuel Martinez paid him in advance to find his brother. He could close the case now and take the money, but it was wrong. Cash aside, Hector deserved to know that Manuel was looking for him. And Rex's brain wouldn't give him a break until he found it.

Another vow to add to his collection: stop taking on seedy cases; stop hurting people; stop drinking. Sometimes it was unclear whether Rex was trying to build a private detective agency or canvass votes for the patron saint of masochism. It seemed every other day he denied himself something else. Rex grabbed his glass of water from the lacquered coffee table and nursed it in his hand, tracing over a tapestry hydrangea with his index finger.

Virginia's sweet giggle stopped. Her chestnut hair bobbed over her shoulders, framing the V-shaped lapels that drew the eye to her cleavage, not that she needed help in that department. Her plump red lips twisted into a devilish grin, which pulled her cheeks high and left the tiniest trace of wrinkles around her mouth. Everything she did seemed to make her more elegant, more alluring. Her lips cracked open, and her husky British accent spilled out like golden champagne, light and intoxicating.

"Rex, darling, you seem a little distant. Did you want a drink? Something to take the edge off."

Virginia leaned over the sofa to the small bar behind the couch and grabbed a bottle of whiskey. The amber liquid inside sparkled under the dimmed lights like molten gold. Rex wanted nothing more than to gargle half the bottle like a fish and wake up the next day without remembering a single thing. A tiny voice in the back of his skull dared him to take it. Where did keeping promises get him? In a dead-end case that hung over his shoulder like a nagging ghost. Surely he was allowed to switch off at the end of the day. His heart pounded in his throat. He clutched his water glass in one hand while the other clamped onto a rough cushion with a white-knuckled grip.

"I'm fine." The last word slipped through his lips an octave too high.

Rex let out a deep, rather unconvincing chuckle, which Virginia probably didn't buy. Instead, she sipped from her glass and inspected him with her hazel eyes before she seemed to bite her tongue and return to her drink.

"So, Suzie really told you she was taking a doctor on a date of hot dogs and a musical? She's a strange little duck, isn't she?"

"It's crazy, right? Musicals are terrible."

Rex placed his glass on the polished coffee table before them, then leaned back into his sofa. The soft cushions enveloped his shoulders. It was the first time he remembered relaxing since the Cinderella case. His muscles turned to jelly as he leaned back and closed his eyes with a sigh.

"I suppose some of them aren't too bad," said Virginia, stroking her chin as though she was being interviewed by the Scoop. "I saw *One Touch of Venus* a few years ago and quite enjoyed it. I think it's the fact that they sing live, or in the case of *Bloomer Girl*, people are amazed if they even sing at all.

"Honestly, it doesn't surprise me. I met Caroline Lake back when I was getting started. It was a terrible picture through Zodiac Studios. *It Came from the Ocean* or some such nonsense. She took me under her wing, but something always seemed a little off, like everything about her was false."

"But she was still your friend?" asked Rex.

She ran a delicate hand over Rex's cheek. "It's sweet how naïve you are sometimes."

Virginia chuckled so hard she snorted, then immediately let out a delicate sigh as she seemed to cover for it. She seemed pretty impressed with her comment, but all Rex could think about was how much press this movie was getting, and if the Cinderella case had taught him anything, there was no such thing as bad publicity in Hollywood.

"But that's not even the best part of my day," Rex tilted his hat over his closed eyes. "This glorified beat cop from Vice meets me over on Skid Row. Turns out I know the kid. He was in the 407th with me. A cocky little brat by the name of Charles Benson. He wanted me to join the LAPD or consult with them or something."

"Maybe you should," said Virginia. "Hear him out, at least."

Rex pulled the hat from his head and sat it on the table. Virginia sprawled over the white sofa in her blue cotton dress, a wide smirk across her red lips.

"Why not?" she tilted her glass in his direction. "Perhaps it isn't wise to make an enemy of this man."

"He would never do anything to me," said Rex. "This kid acts like he rules the town, but you never truly forget the chain of command. Even he understands that."

"Then there's nothing but benefits to having the Los Angeles police on your side. I could only imagine how differently things might have turned out if we had the LAPD come with us to the Oakwood Lot a couple of months ago. It might've been a little less dramatic, but I might not have been held hostage."

"Come on." Rex lowered his voice to a hoarse whisper. "I saved the day, didn't I?"

"Yes, you did."

Virginia shuffled across the sofa and climbed onto Rex's lap. She leaned in so close, and Rex breathed the floral notes of Chanel No. 5 on her creamy white skin, mingling with the piney scent of gin on her breath. Part of him, a dark part he would never utter a word about, thrummed with excitement at the smell, and he wanted to kiss her more. They curled their arms around one another and slowly leaned in. Eyes closed, Virginia's soft lips, like two silky caterpillars, glided over his own, sending a tingle down his spine. She pressed her lips against his, and they locked in a passionate kiss, which felt worthy of ending some four-hour silver screen epic.

Virginia pulled back and placed a hand on his chest. "You know, I *would* sleep a lot better knowing that you had some backup out there. They might call this place the City of Angels, but it's filled with wolves and thieves that would cut your throat for so little as a single shilling. That thought terrifies me. It keeps me up at night when you're out there on one of your stakes."

"Stakeouts," Rex corrected. "And trust me, Benson is the biggest wolf of them all. You haven't seen this kid in action. He pulled a gun on a reporter and threatened to frame him by putting heroin in his car if he didn't stop asking questions about you."

"Well." Virginia smirked with a cutesy eye roll. "Sounds to me like Mr. Benson understands how to defend a lady's honor. Chivalry isn't dead after all."

"Virginia, this is serious. He's dangerous."

"But you said so yourself. The kid would never do anything to you. You were his captain."

"Major," Rex corrected. "But that's not important. He's a petulant little kid who only gets people killed. And now that same reckless child is working for Vice."

Virginia sighed. "All I'm saying is—"

"And I'm telling you the kid is no good, end of story."

Virginia climbed off his lap and shuffled across the sofa as far as she could. "I was only trying to help."

Anger still pumped through Rex's veins. He pursed his lips and let out a long sigh.

"Look, you don't know him the way I do. He was the reason I ended up where I did in France." Rex grabbed his water glass and chugged, but it didn't have the same bite as his usual gin and tonic (hold the tonic.)

"You mean when..." Virginia paused as she seemed to choose her following words carefully. "You mean that dreadful accident in the war."

"I'd rather not talk about it."

Virginia slurped the last mouthful of gin with an audible gulp, then tapped the glass with her red nails. She stared at him for a few beats, her eyes darting from the unused fireplace to the framed photos on the whitewashed wood-paneled walls. It seemed as though she wanted to give anything her attention but him. Heat radiated from Rex's cheeks. What hare-brained story had she concocted in her head?

"It wasn't all bad," Virginia's voice came out in a whisper.

"Seriously?" Rex arched an eyebrow. "I've been dreaming about bullets and plane crashes since 1916. That I could live with, but what happened to that kid was unspeakable."

"I'm not saying the act itself wasn't horrific." Virginia paused. "But you must admit some good has come from it."

"Good! You realize that boy is laying in a box in some French cemetery because of me. His family probably still don't know where he is. I don't even know why I decided to tell you about that." Rex slammed his drink on the desk and groaned upright, undercutting his authority, but he stood tall to salvage his remaining dignity.

"I'm not saying I'm glad you did it. I'm not a monster."

"Unlike me, is that it?" Rex groaned.

"Now, just stop that." Virginia pointed her index finger at him. "All I am saying is perhaps you could look at this as a silver lining. Those horrible events have already transpired, and nothing will change that. But they changed you into the kind, considerate man you are now."

Rex hobbled around the sofa and stopped at the shimmering glasses laid before him on the modest bar. Sweat beaded on his forehead as he clutched a whiskey glass with a trembling hand. He thumbed the sharp pyramids cut into a pattern around the glass. Bottles of alcohol stood proudly, the colors of gold and honey; each one medicine for his soul.

"I worry about you, that's all." Virginia rested her chin on the couch's back.

Heat tightened in Rex's throat. He clamped his lips shut, but the words clawed up his throat and dribbled out like hot bile.

"Maybe next time, you should keep your nose out of things that have nothing to do with you."

Virginia shot to her feet and staggered back as the gin seemed to rush to her head. She straightened her blue dress and shook a strand of chestnut hair from her eyes with a sigh. A blatant attempt to retain the dignity the gin hadn't already robbed from her.

"Which cinema did you say Suzie was going to?" Virginia's lips soured into a sneer. "After all, even some second-rate musical has to be more fun than this."

Virginia strode across the room with a hammy gait that would put Scarlett O'Hara to shame. She seemed to lap every second of it, even pacing herself up the steps. What was the deluded actress waiting for? Surely she didn't expect Rex to come crawling back to her after she threw his darkest shame back in his face. Rex regretted selling his apartment. It might have been a barely liveable hovel over a pharmacy, but he had a place to go. Still, he couldn't be in the house with that woman.

Virginia glided up a couple more stairs before she turned back, tears glistening in her eyes, no doubt a not-so-subtle manipulation she learned in her years as a professional liar. She slid her fingers along the polished banister and smiled.

"This whole argument," Virginia flashed her porcelain-white teeth, which forced a tear to roll down her cheek at the perfect moment. "It's all been so preposterous. How about we go upstairs to bed together. Then in the morning, we will look back at this silly incident and laugh."

Rex twisted the glossy glass in his hand, breathed deep, then placed it back on the bar. There was only one way he was getting through a night with Virginia, and it involved wiping the slate clean with enough gin to take down a circus elephant. He grabbed his homburg hat from the sofa and placed it on his head.

"Where are you going?" Virginia screamed.

Rex turned to face the actress. Her lips split open enough to see a hint of teeth, just enough for her to appear vulnerable.

"I'll give you a chance to sleep this off," Rex grumbled. "If you need me, I'll be at the office."

Chapter 4

Rex's brand-new mint-green Pontiac Torpedo tore along the Hollywood Freeway. The detective's foot leaned against the pedal like a dirty cop on a perp. A crisp wind flicked his silver hair through the open window as he checked the clock-style speedometer.

Forty-five miles an hour.

Adrenaline pumped through his body like gasoline through the engine, fuelling the bitterness combusting in his chest. The ivory steering wheel creaked under his sweaty fingers as he tightened his grip. Virginia wouldn't be satisfied until he became a crooked cop like Benson.

Over a shrub-dotted hill, a bright light scrubbed out the night sky from The Hollywood Bowl, nestled in the desert hills. Probably a crooner like Frank Sinatra or some classically trained pianist nobody knew. Worse yet, it could've been another ill-conceived musical, like the awful rendition of *Oklahoma!* that closed at the Bowl after only two performances a month ago.

A tingle burrowed under Rex's skin like some exotic parasite, chewing at his insides as he pictured Suzie and her doctor date at the theater, enduring *Bloomer Girl*. While he wished Suzie well, it wasn't like he was hinging everything on the budding relationship.

He didn't even know the man. Still, something about the musical made his blood boil. If he was honest, the singing-dancing morons on the screen were nothing more than punching bags for him to vent his aggression.

The car in front of Rex slowed down to thirty miles an hour. He tooted his horn, but the driver puttered along as though he was the only one on the road. The detective wrenched the wheel to the right, and the car jerked into the next lane. He kicked the gas. The eight-cylinder engine thundered under the hood as he charged on, and the Torpedo ripped past the driver: an old crone with coke bottle glasses, hunched over the wheel like it was the only thing stopping her from toppling over. Rex pounded his horn three times and shouted, "Move it, grandma! Learn how to drive or get off the damn road!"

As Rex turned onto Vine Street, his bubbling stomach progressed to a burn in the back of his throat, like the words were clawing up his esophagus. Words he should've told Virginia.

"A good thing," he mumbled to himself.

Further proof they came from different worlds. Virginia lived in a fantasy. Not everything needed to have a deeper meaning, like one of her sappy pictures. The kid's death wasn't part of some grand plan. It was Rex's mistake, but the kid was the one who slowly bled out. And then there was the girl, screaming his name on repeat.

"Felix," her voice echoed.

Rex only watched the kid's girlfriend, or maybe it was his sister, on the checkered floor as she clutched the boy's blood-smeared hand and watched the life slip from his eyes as he gargled like a slowly draining bathtub.

Red lights flashed behind him.

Bright headlights followed him along Vine, followed by a shrill wail. A black and white paddy wagon roared after him in the rear view.

"You've got to be kidding me," Rex's voice rumbled as he pulled up outside Wallichs Music City. A block away from his office, the closed store lit up like a beacon that shone over the last intersection before he was home. Just when he thought the fight with Virginia was rock bottom, the floor dropped out under him, and he discovered a new layer of sediment to sink to. The detective dropped his head against the steering wheel. A door slammed behind. The shape stood in front of the car with the unmistakable silhouette of a cop hat.

"Put your hands on the steering wheel, sir."

Rex did as ordered. Fate had dished an ice-cold slab of life on his plate, and he wasn't looking for seconds.

"I'm a private investigator," Rex shouted. "My office is just—"

"Quiet, sir," the police officer called out.

Rex closed his eyes and imagined Benson was the cop that pulled him over, even though Vice was too important to concern themselves with an insignificant traffic ticket. But Rex indulged the daydream as the Vice cop would tell him not to worry about it and maybe caution Rex just to stroke his ego, but the whole thing would be nothing more than a formality.

The fantasy was lovely and all, and perhaps it would be nice to drop Benson's name and have a single win to cap off the day. Even if he could, Rex was no better than Benson if he expected the world to cave to his every whim because he had a terrible day. So Rex gritted his teeth and smiled as the young cop who wasn't Benson approached the Pontiac. The kid seemed barely old enough to shave. Had they lowered the LAPD retiring age to twenty-five?

"This ride is killer diller," said the kid cop.

"Uh, thanks," Rex mumbled.

"I've always wanted a Pontiac, you know," the policeman chuckled, leaning against the car, though Rex wasn't going to tell him to remove his greasy paws off the fresh paintwork. "But with a wife and a kid on the way, I don't think I'll be seeing one of these babies anytime soon."

"It—" Rex cleared his throat. "It's a very nice car."

"But look, I've still gotta book you. Do you realize you were going at—" The policeman beamed his flashlight through the driver's window. "Hold on a minute. You're him, aren't you?"

Rex's stomach sunk. He just wanted the speeding fine, so he could go back and end the god-forsaken day. Was that too much to ask? His best chance was to play dumb, and the cop seemed just dense enough to buy it.

"I don't know what you're talking about," said Rex.

"Yeah, I remember you. You're the one that solved the Cinderella case. The one that thinks he's a cop all of a sudden because he got lucky. Once. Trying to steal our jobs, are you?"

Rex dry swallowed and flattened his hands over the steering wheel.

The police officer dropped his torch to reveal a broad smile before he burst into cackles of laughter. Rex chuckled along with the maniac. The last thing he wanted to do was piss off another looney cop with a gun, or his rock bottom day might be his last.

"Take it easy, Horne. I'm just busting your chops. Every time you solve a case, it's less work for me. How about we chalk this one up to a mistake and let you go with a warning."

"No!" Rex shouted, leaning out the car window, then snapping his hands against the steering wheel as the police officer reached for his revolver as Rex may have got a little too comfortable. "Sorry, I didn't mean to raise my voice. I don't want any special treatment. Did Benson put you up to this?"

"Who?" The policeman shook his head. "Listen, sir, you're a first-timer, and I'm going to let you off with a warning."

Rex bit the inside of his cheek. There was every chance the officer was playing dumb (and doing an outstanding job of it.) Maybe Benson was still pulling the strings to show Rex how cozy it could be if he got into bed with the Police Department.

"Look, I'm not trying to cause trouble or anything, but can you just give me the ticket."

"You're the boss." The policeman sighed and shook his head as he pulled out his flipbook, scribbling down the ticket.

Strange elation washed over him in an icy sweat. Who would've thought that he would be relieved to end his day with a speeding fine? He might be slower to get results, but at least his vow ensured that he got them legitimately. He would land in jail before letting Benson drag him into old habits.

A small price to pay.

The crinkled hundred-dollar bill crunched in Rex's fingers as he straightened it with his thumb. Strips of orange streetlight illuminated Benjamin Franklin's grease-dappled face. Almost like the puddles of blood splattered under Mr. Martinez's pale corpse.

Rex flattened the battered banknote on his polished mahogany desk. For a guy like Martinez, scrimping and grifting his way across Skid Row, it must've taken a lifetime to squirrel away his relative fortune. Still, he handed it over, trusting Rex to find his brother.

Rex insisted on payment upfront, but now the man's brother had disappeared into the ether, and it was hardly like he could refund the man. There was only one real solution.

Another alternative soaked through his brain like an oil spill, creeping over the folds like black tentacles. He could always drop the do-gooder act and admit that he wasn't any better than those bums and low lives. What would half the people on Skid Row do when things got too hard, and everything collapsed in on them? They could grab a bottle of bourbon or whiskey and would drink until they couldn't remember their terrible lives.

Rex groaned out of his swivel chair and plodded to the painting of a red maple-lined suburban street on the wall, dotted with cars and white picket fences, much like the house where Rex grew up.

Rex lost count of the times he dragged his mother inside off the stoop because one of her gentleman callers dumped the evil shrew like last week's garbage. It certainly didn't excuse his mother's behavior, but Rex had been there. Knowing his mother's fate was a further incentive to stay away from that poison.

Despite this, an ache rumbled in his gut. Throat dry. Cold sweats. Every cell in his brain begged him not to repeat his mother's mistakes and, if he was honest, his own. The rest of his body quaked with anticipation at that first smooth sip. With a shaky hand, he removed the painting from the wall and set it on the floor, then twisted the dial of the safe behind it until he heard a click. He heaved the iron door open. Inside, a cloth bag half-filled with cash rested beside an equally full bottle of Fleischmann's Gin.

Suzie had been through the office like a colonel through a private's quarters, removing contraband, but she didn't have access to the safe. Rex should've thrown the damn bottle away; she was right to remove temptation, but part of him probably never truly believed that he would ever honestly give up the booze.

He stashed the crinkled note in the cloth bag and returned it to the safe, but his hand lingered inside. He brushed his fingers over the smooth curves of the bottle. Then remembering every painful moment of the day, he grabbed it and returned to his desk.

He sat down in his swivel chair, opened the second drawer, rifled through the junk, and pulled out an old black and white photo. Two rows of men posed at the airbase, one standing, one crouched down, smiles on all their faces. But the rows of beaming grins only served as a reminder that almost half of the 407th never made it back. Benson sat front and center, probably at his insistence. *Of course* he would've insisted. Another soldier leaned against his Spitfire in the corner, his jet-black hair slicked back, a cocky smirk stretched across his face.

"Holloway," Rex murmured. "God, I wish you were here right now. You'd know what to do. You wouldn't have hesitated. You would've decked the little prick for talking down to me."

Rex smiled at the photo, but then his face sagged. He snatched the Fleischmann's bottle and twisted the cap off. The piney scent of juniper berries wafted into his nostrils, just like the hint that was on Virginia's breath. Rex closed his eyes, savoring those few seconds before he opened them. Rex glanced between Holloway's smirk and Benson's glib grin. He placed the photograph on the desk and gripped the bottle with two hands.

"Lord, give me strength."

Chapter 5

A keen pang in Rex's cricked neck yanked him from a dreamless sleep. He peeked through tired eyes but pinched them shut as a white light drenched the room. The detective reached out a hand and patted the desk to climb up, but his hand knocked something hard, followed by a sharp thump, which jolted him upright.

The empty Fleischmann's bottle rocked on its side on the floor, a jagged crack running from the long neck down to underneath the yellow label. He stared at the empty bottle as his heart still pounded from the noise until somebody rapped on the office door.

Rex pivoted in his swivel chair as the door creaked open.

"Mr. H, what happened?" Suzie held a hand over her mouth as she let out a dramatic gasp. "You look like hell."

"Thanks for the medical assessment, Suzie." Rex straightened up his grey suit, as though that would make him any less of a spectacle.

Suzie chuckled. Her eyes dropped to the glass bottle on the floorboards and the Cheshire Cat smile wilted, shrinking into a thin line as she marched inside, her hands on her hips.

"Where do you think you get off, getting back on that hooch." Suzie's Jersey accent kicked into gear with the word off and only got thicker from there. "I already lost a job here once because of your love of the booze, and I won't let it happen again."

"Suzie," Rex groaned. "Take it easy. I didn't get a whole lot of sleep last night."

"I'll bet." She scoffed. "If you think I'm gonna stand by and watch you drink yourself into an early grave, then you've got another thing coming, Mister. My uncle was like you. He—"

Rex raised a hand, and the receptionist staggered back with an indignant glare. Rex took the small window of silence to jump in and explain.

"I'm tired, Suzie, that's all. I was up late, racking my brains to solve this Martinez case. I'd be lying if I said I didn't want a drink, but I poured it out the window. The alley cat I accidentally spilled it on wasn't pleased about it, but that's it."

The chipper grin slowly returned to Suzie's mouth. "Oh, Mr. H, I knew you wouldn't really go through with it."

"Yet you shouted at me anyway," Rex scoffed.

Suzie tittered with a cutesy grin. "What made you stay here overnight? You fight with Virginia?"

"How did your date with Doctor David go?" Rex flashed Suzie a fat smile.

"It was lovely." Suzie smiled, but her eyes narrowed on him like a cheetah about to pounce on its prey. "Thank you for asking."

"You sure that musical didn't scare him off?" Rex teased, anything to deflect from the topic of Virginia.

"A cute little picture. It gave me a bit of a giggle when Caroline Lake started singing. She scrunched her face and squeezed like she was pushing out the notes, but you could tell it wasn't her."

"Nothing about that woman is real." A smooth voice came from behind Suzie.

A woman stepped through the office door in a grey skirt and fur-trimmed jacket. She tilted her head under her wide-brimmed hat. The sepia-skinned woman's round face offered a rehearsed smile.

"I'm sorry, who are you?" asked Rex.

The woman didn't answer. She took a deep breath and belted out "Evalina," with a cutesy little squeak at the end. Suzie's jaw dropped, and she turned to Rex with an open-mouthed grin as though he was supposed to know what the singing was, or perhaps she was just happy the madwoman proved Rex wrong that crazy people do burst into song.

"This is her," Suzie squeaked. "Billie Bailey, the singer from Bloomer Girl. The one Caroline Lake—"

"I get the picture," said Rex. "Why don't you give us a moment?"

"I saw your movie last night, Miss Bailey." Suzie rushed to the woman's side and took her by the hand.

The singer snatched her hand back, turned her nose at Suzie, and strode past her.

"It isn't my movie," Billie Bailey's velvety voice ran cold. "That woman bought my voice for a buck, and I accepted it because she promised she had the connections to advance my singing career, and all she needed was my voice."

Rex rose from his swivel chair, trying one last-ditch effort at straightening his clothes.

"Suzie." He cleared his throat.

"Message received, boss."

Suzie fled from the office, although Rex figured it was less obedience to her employer and more to escape the awkward situation. She closed the door behind her with a gentle click. Rex rose from his desk and gestured towards the chair opposite.

"Please, have a seat."

She nodded. "Thank you."

The woman sauntered across the office with the grace of a Geisha, as though she walked on a cloud. She lowered herself into the chair, resting her hands in her lap. Her perfect smile caved in on itself.

"I don't even know where to begin." Her voice tightened on the last word.

Billie pulled a bone-white handkerchief from her sleeve and dabbed it against her thick lashes.

"Why don't you start with what happened," said Rex, which came out a little cold, but he wasn't sure how else to get the ball moving with what little information she gave him?

"My husband is Carl Bailey," she sniffed. "We run The Neptune Lounge just down the street. Carl managed the money, and I sang. That's where she came in. Caroline must've heard about me somewhere, so she visited the club."

"And how did that go?"

"Have you ever heard of an anglerfish?"

Rex shook his head with a shrug.

"Daddy was a fisherman, the king of the sea they used to call him. He told me about these fish at the bottom of the ocean, where it's pitch black. It's just darkness all the time. These angler fish light up, and the other little fish see it. It entices them in with this little twinkle and when it finally has them reeled in."

Mrs. Bailey snapped her hands together, mimicking the creature's jaws.

"And that's what she did to you?"

"I actually thought she was kind." Mrs. Bailey scoffed. "Promised me a life of fame and fortune, which I didn't even want. I was happy doing my lounge shows, but she was very persuasive."

"Actors can be that way," Rex muttered.

"She said she would only pay me one dollar. That was it. But she said she had contacts, people that would get me a singing contract. She promised she had friends at every record label from Elektra to Atlantic."

Billie shook her head and chewed her lip. Rex's heart turned to concrete, but there was nothing he could do for the woman.

"I'm sorry, Mrs. Bailey, truly I am." Rex held a hand over his heart. "But unfortunately, so many actors will lie, cheat and steal to get what they want."

"Odd thing to say as someone who is dating a star."

Rex's heart dropped into his gut. He hadn't forgiven Virginia for her ridiculous comments about Benson. Still, he couldn't air their dirty laundry to a woman he had just met.

"I didn't say all." He cleared his throat. "At the end of the day, we can't do anything about the fact that she cheated you out of a small fortune."

"That's not why I'm here," Mrs. Bailey paused for a moment. "The money and fame weren't enough for her. She had to take him too."

"You mean your husband?"

"He wasn't home when I woke up this morning, and I didn't think much of it. I assumed he went to do some paperwork at the club, but when I got there, one of our waiters found a note."

She handed him a crumpled piece of yellow paper. Rex flattened it out and read it to himself; he wasn't going to be callous enough to read it aloud.

Bill,

Things haven't been working with us for a while. Caroline sees me as more than a working partner. She sees me as a man, as a sexual being. She makes me feel the way you did all those years ago. You never look at me like you used to, and when I touch you, you act like my fingers are made of ice.

I know this might hurt for a little, but deep down, you know you don't care about me like you used to. Let's go our separate ways. And after this whole musical headache, I'm taking Caroline to her house in San Francisco.

Wishing you the best,

Carl.

"Always the poet," the jilted woman sobbed into her handkerchief.

"I'm sorry," said Rex.

"And the worst part is, it's my fault."

"Don't say that."

"No, it is," she said. "I saw her moving in on him, and so I made sure The Hollywood Scoop knew the truth about Miss Lake's performance. I wanted to hurt her, and maybe I thought that if the news exposed her, Carl would see her for what she was. But obviously, I only pushed him into her arms."

An uncomfortable tingle rose under Rex's collar as the woman wept into her hands at the desk. Rex felt terrible for the woman's situation, but it bothered him when she started crying. He had never done well with emotions, and after a childhood loaded with his mother's dramatic and sometimes downright violent outbursts, he became numb to the wails and sobs; they even made him angry at times.

He hated himself for it.

"I'm sorry for your loss," said Rex.

"He didn't die." The *former* Mrs. Bailey rolled her tear-slicked eyes. "That's why I want you to find him, so that I can drag him back."

Deja vu washed over Rex. He couldn't count the times jilted wives sat in this office, begging him to surveil her husband, only to find out what she feared all along. Even if she managed to track him and the other woman down, the only person who won in that scenario was Rex. But he was done with that kind of seedy private eye schtick. With all the notoriety that the Cinderella case brought, he could make a real difference and not take on that kind of low-hanging fruit.

"I'm not sure you want to do this," said Rex.

"With all due respect Mr. Horne, you don't know me."

"Probably better than you think," said Rex. "Let's say you find him, and then what? You yell at him a little? Drag him back home by his ear like a naughty child. I've seen this story before, a lot, and it never ends well."

"You're not like other private detectives, are you?"

"Not anymore." Rex shrugged.

"Look, Mr. Horne, I can't eat. I'm sure I won't be able to sleep tonight. All I can think of is where my husband is. Knowing can't be as bad as waiting for him to come through the door. Please, I'm begging you to find him."

Desperation sparkled in the woman's eyes. Her full lips with a soft cupid's bow sagged a little. Rex leaned back in his chair. Perhaps it was kinder to give the woman some solace in knowing precisely what happened. Though all he saw was the explosion of emotion, at least those women knew the truth.

"I normally charge three dollars an hour plus expenses," said Rex, hoping the cost might deter her from what would likely be throwing her money away.

"The Neptune Lounge is doing fine right now, Mr. Horne," said Mrs. Bailey. "You needn't worry about money."

"Fine," Rex sighed. "But there are going to be a couple of ground rules."

Mrs. Bailey shrugged. "Naturally."

"When we find them, and we will find them, you cannot get involved."

"I am his wife."

"I understand that." Rex held up a hand. "But, when we find them, they will most likely be together, playing happy families. At that moment, you are probably going to want to scream at her and ask her why, or maybe you wanna scratch her eyes out. She might even say things to try and tempt you, but you cannot react."

"Can I at least speak with my husband?" Mrs. Bailey flailed her handkerchief in the air.

"Of course, but it needs to stay calm," said Rex. "I've seen this too many times before. You expect that he will come running back to you because you decided to run after him. He *will* most likely stay with her, and you need to be prepared to accept that. What he did was pretty crummy, but it's not illegal."

"I think I can do that."

"You think?"

"I can," said Billie.

"Well, in that case." Rex rose from his chair. "I think we need to head down to your club and speak with this employee."

Chapter 6

The Neptune Lounge sat two blocks from Rex's office. The narrow hall stretched back at least one hundred feet to a modest stage with a silver microphone and phonograph on a wooden stool. Warm light bounced off the golden art deco patterns that glittered on the maroon carpet, their beauty sabotaged by the heavy odor of stale cigar smoke. Seated at one of the thirty or so circular tables crammed across the space, Rex picked at the linen tablecloth as he nursed the whiskey Billie poured him before she hovered around the chamber like a worker bee. She currently grinned, chatting to a delivery man.

The club's head waiter, Marco Rossi, sat opposite Rex in his crisp tuxedo, arms folded. He seemed to make great efforts to conceal his right hand, which Rex suspected was to hide the deformed pinky he noticed when Mr. Rossi sat down.

"Fridges died," Rossi explained. "Damn rat chewed through the cables. Just another thing she has to deal with along with that broken lock on the liquor cabinet and a missing husband, but she'd be too nice to tell you any of that, and you'd probably be too selfish to care."

"Have I done something to you?" asked Rex. "She asked me to help."

"Mrs. Bailey works her fingers to the bone. Now you're going to slink in here like a whipsnake, taking that hard-earned cash from her by telling her what she already knows."

"I tried to tell her."

"Well, try harder." Marco pounded his fist on the table, cleared his throat, and straightened the fabric as the *waiter mask* settled back on his face. "She loves Carl and would do anything for him, but that's what they do, isn't it?"

"Who?"

"Battered wives."

"He smacks her around?" Rex pulled his flipbook from his pocket and scribbled notes.

"They live upstairs. Sometimes I would stay back to tidy up, and I would hear them both up there. Those horrible crashes and the screams."

Rex glanced at the woman on the small stage. She managed the same rehearsed smile she did for Suzie. It seemed almost second nature to her, like she had spent a long time, maybe her whole life, playing a role. Had her relationship with her husband crushed the genuine joy out of her? Or was it the life of a lounge singer and the seedy underbelly that came with that?

"I just need to be able to give Mrs. Bailey reassurance."

Although Rex wasn't sure who needed consolation after the waiter dredged up a host of doubts: was he kidding himself? Taking on the case wasn't a moral choice; more than likely, it was a chance to pat himself on the back as he slid into old habits. He couldn't afford to go down that rabbit hole, especially with a glass of whiskey within reach.

He cleared his throat. "I have already hashed this out with Mrs. Bailey. We have agreed this is simply about finding the information to know what happened. You found the note. I need to confirm it was Mr. Bailey's handwriting; to rule out any foul play."

"Carl could be laying in a ditch somewhere for all I care," the waiter spat the words like the most bitter cough syrup. "The important thing you need to do is make sure that he doesn't come back. Mrs. Bailey has a chance to move on with her life because if that bum comes back, they will have a back and forth, and everyone will think it's some screwball comedy act like *His Girl Friday*, but when the sun goes down, those crashes and bangs will be ringing up there."

The waiter pointed to the crown-molded ceiling.

"Now, if we're done, I need to replace the tablecloths."

The slightest tear appeared on the white fabric when Rex lifted his hand from where he had been scratching. Rex stood and grabbed the man's hand, placing three one-dollar bills in it.

"Sorry," he said.

The man tossed the cash to the table. "I don't want your money or your pity. All I want from you, no matter what you find, is to tell Mrs. Bailey that Carl left with that talentless shrew. Maybe they left for Austin or Dallas. Hell, I don't care if they left for Venezuela. It doesn't matter. Just make them disappear."

The waiter stormed off, bumping past another man in a white shirt and woolen sweater, his hair slicked back with enough pomade to drown a mountain lion, and could probably choke it to death from the stench of vanilla and tobacco that wafted his way.

The man offered Rex a wink as he approached the boxy microphone at the front of the stage. Beside it, the man tinkered, sliding a wax cylinder onto the phonograph, clipping it in. A dull rendition of a sharp piano pattern blossomed into a complex melody that rang throughout the hall. The man hummed as he approached the silver microphone and started singing about a woman named Evalina. Rex hobbled to his feet and approached the stage as the tempo grew faster. The man shot him a smile as though he had a captive audience, but Rex was more interested in his song choice. If he were a simple employee of the Neptune Lounge, then surely Mrs. Bailey would have put the kybosh on that song; any reminder of Caroline Lake was sure to be banned, or at the least in *very* poor taste.

Although it still seemed insensitive, it must've been some co-star from the film. The singer grew louder as the piano roared into a crescendo, then petered off into a simple melody before it finished.

Rex clapped, and the man bowed before him. Entertainers, they were all so easy to please. Throw a little attention their way, and they were eating from your palm like an animal in a petting zoo.

"Have you seen *Bloomer Girl* yet?"

Rex shrugged. "Haven't had the chance. Are you in it?"

"How stupid of me," the man gave a seemingly honest chuckle that threw Rex off guard. "Jimmy Evans. I'm a singer mostly, but - *Bloomer Girl* was my first job in the movies."

The crooner crossed his arms and smirked. It was as though on paper the man should come across as a smarmy pain in the neck like all the others, but he carried himself like any man you might pass on the street. The whole scene took Rex a moment to absorb before he continued questioning.

"And that's how you know Mrs. Bailey?"

The man nodded, his broad grin effortlessly stretched across his face.

"I met her when I first came in with Caroline Lake. Oh, it was a lovely night. She performed a slow jazz version of *It's Been a Long, Long Time*. Honestly, it put Kitty Kallen to shame."

Rex offered a nod. The only thing he wanted to do was follow up about Caroline Lake and if he had heard anything about them. But if the man caught a waft of Rex interrogating him, he might fly like a vampire before garlic.

"I haven't heard her sing."

"She is the cat's pajamas, let me tell you." Evans sighed.

Rex hesitated, taking a moment to glance at the crown molding. It seemed an outlandish theory, but it was too early in the case to rule out anything. If Mr. Bailey had a history of violence, there was a chance Caroline Lake had thrown a trademark actor temper tantrum, and suddenly, she wasn't an exotic mistress anymore. Perhaps she threatened him, and he decided to correct things; maybe things got a little out of hand, and now he was lying low trying to figure out what to do with the body of the most talked-about actress in Hollywood. Or perhaps the Cinderella case had let his imagination run wild. Still, he needed to pursue every avenue.

"What about her husband?" asked Rex. "Did you get to meet him?"

"Hideous man." Jimmy Evans shook his head. "But, as our lord tells us, I turned the other cheek."

While the man retained his Sunday service demeanor, his body tensed at the mention of Carl Bailey. Even the silent religious types had their limits. The crooner's skin turned a waxy shade of tapioca white, and his smile twitched. There was a story inside the man, and unfortunately for him, Rex would extract it like a rotted tooth.

"And what makes Carl Bailey so hideous."

"It was when we first met as I already told you," Mr. Evans paused, as though he seemed to justify what would come next. "And I said exactly what I said to you. I complimented his wife on her song, and he near knocked the heck out of me for it. Said I was hitting on his woman."

While Carl Bailey wouldn't be the first man to fly into a jealous rage, something about the picture of the club owner didn't seem to gel. His words in the letter oozed with poetry; while it might not have been Yeates, it was honest and emotional, whereas the man Evans described seemed more like the man Rex tried so hard not to be. Shoot first and ask questions later.

The letter had a definite feminine flavor. Assuming the cagey waiter did see Mr. Bailey's handwriting, that didn't prove the actress wasn't in his ear, instructing him with the perfect words to abandon his marriage like some sick version of *Cyrano de Bergerac*.

"So, he was violent with you?" asked Rex.

"You could say that," said Evans. "I know I shouldn't say this about a missing person, but I hope he stays lost with Caroline. Those two deserve each other."

"Did Miss Lake do something to you too?" Rex inquired.

The singer paused for a moment, with a faint twinkle in his eye that suggested he understood Rex's implication. But then he flashed Rex his usual smile.

"For a second there, I thought you were saying—"

"You thought what?" pushed Rex.

"It's nothing." He rolled his eyes. "What were we talking about?"

"Caroline Lake," said Rex. "You had a run-in?"

"Nothing like that," Evans dismissed with a wave of his hand. "Caroline just had a reputation, that's all. She was like a spoiled child. If she wanted something, you had two choices. Either you gave her exactly what she wanted and when, or you weathered the storm she would unleash on you."

"Not a fan, I take it."

"Manners cost nothing, you know." Evans shrugged. "I don't care who you are. I've sold millions of records across this country, but it doesn't give me the right to walk around like I'm our Lord almighty."

Perhaps Rex had misjudged the man, or maybe the holy crooner act was a farce to further his selfish career like all actors. Still, Evans smiled at him like a friendly neighbor in some midwestern suburb. It felt genuine.

"That's why I had to let people know the truth. It was the right thing to do. As the good book says, 'And you will know the truth, and the truth will set you free.' John 8:32."

Jimmy Evans shook his head as he stared off into the distance.

"Mrs. Bailey deserves the credit for that angelic voice."

"But wait." Rex held up a hand. "Mrs. Bailey told me she was the one that let everybody know."

"I said I was the reason it got out."

Mrs. Bailey returned in her glittering gold dress, her hair tied up in an elaborate bun around her head. Gentle hints of frangipani and sandalwood followed her as she entered with a cherry-red smile.

"I never said it came from my mouth. If I did that, the studio could sue me for money I never got. Whereas Mr. Evans is a major star. They need him. They wouldn't dare go after him."

"And it was the right thing to do," Mr. Evans repeated.

"Yes, that too, of course."

The right thing to do seemed to be the furthest thing from Mrs. Bailey's mind. Could Rex really blame her? As angry as he was, if some young buck tried to steal Virginia from him, who knows what dark lengths he would go to prove himself as the better man?

"Mr. Evans," said Rex. "Are you still in contact with any of the other cast and crew of *Bloomer Girl*? I want to speak with some people to get a better idea of Miss Lake so we can try to hunt her down."

"Not really, but I'm more than happy to help any way I can." Evans stopped and scratched his chin before he said, "There were those other two, the composers. Altman? No Aldridge. Those two were closest to Caroline, they were inseparable on the set. I'll see if I can get you their numbers."

Chapter 7

Rex mentally pieced the story in his mind, seeing which parts would click in place as he drove down Wilshire Boulevard into Brentwood. The harder he jammed them together, the less they stuck. The possessive husband with an animalistic temper, the battered wife, tossed aside like week-old garbage, and the bible-thumping crooner with a heart of gold. Three different stories that didn't share a decent common thread aside from a few tenuous links to some terrible musical.

The detective pulled over outside the Brentwood Theater. A marquee protruded from the whitewashed building. Even in the middle of the day, the blue and pink neon lights flashed, framing the black letters, which read:

BLOOMER GIRL: THE MOVIE EVERYONE IS TALKING ABOUT

Rex got out of the Pontiac, checked the address scribbled on the crumpled scrap of paper in his pocket, then turned around. Across the street from the empty lot beside the theater sat a five-story apartment complex—the Cordelia. A grey brick cube with fire escapes dribbling between the seemingly endless rows of windows. The sterile box seemed like the kind of place the so-called *Hollywood elite* like to infest. He shuddered at all the false smiles and stilted hugs he would endure, then breathed deep and hobbled across the busy street.

The lobby had more trimmings than a thanksgiving dinner. Marble floors so polished you could comb your hair in them; pure white sofas so plush you didn't want to sit; even a modest indoor fountain, if there was such a thing. Immaculately dressed men and women, all of which at least half his age, strolled out as though posing for a pamphlet. Rex seemed like a craggy geezer in his usual cotton suit. He fought the urge to roll his eyes.

No apartment building was that fun.

Rex strolled over to reception, avoiding the myriad of sideways stares and hushed murmurs. The kid in a maroon suit behind the marble counter beamed at him with a smile so painfully tight Rex half expected it to snap like an overextended rubber band.

"How can I help you on this glorious afternoon, sir?"

"I'm here to meet with Betty and Bernard Aldridge."

"And they are expecting you?" the bellhop asked.

Rex twinged at the kid's words. Perhaps he was still a little on edge after the last twenty-four hours, but it seemed the bellhop's manner implied he was a liar. But what was he to do? Punch the little bastard's lights out and break his vow because *he didn't like his tone?*

"I called them an hour ago," said Rex through gritted teeth.

A slappable smile still stretched across his face, the brat picked up the gold-trimmed receiver on the desk and dialed, then glanced at the ceiling as he waited for a response.

"Ah, Mr. Aldridge, I have a man to see you. Goes by the name of Mr.—" The bellhop snapped his fingers at Rex, and in turn, Rex bit the inside of his cheek. The only thing he could do to not rip the kid's fingers off and shove them where the sun didn't shine.

"Rex Horne." Rex's voice lowered to a growl.

"Mr. Horne," said the arrogant child, slick as Valvoline. "Excellent, sir. I will send him up immediately."

The attendant hung up the phone and cleared his throat as he shuffled a few papers around the desk. He probably looked forward to booting an old coot like Rex out on his ear. That'd make him a big man. But the little brat didn't count on Rex telling the truth. Judging from the pinched expression on his face, it tore the little prick up inside. Rex smirked.

"Thank you so much," he said, mirroring the bellhop's over-the-top excitement. "You have been a tremendous help."

The attendant's smile dropped from his face, and he marched Rex over to the elevators across the foyer. He gestured for Rex to step inside, and Rex obliged. The kid went in after him, placed a key into the hole below the gold-buttoned panel, turned it with a clunk, and pressed the button for level five.

"Don't trust me?" asked Rex.

"It is the penthouse level," the bellhop snapped. "You cannot get in without a key."

The elevator took off with a hum. Seconds later, the gold doors slid open on a blue-grey apartment stuffed with matching floral furniture and a grand piano in the corner. Betty and Bernard stood side by side, smiling at him, like something out of a Sears catalog. Their freckled alabaster skin looked as though it had never seen sunlight, which stood out in a sun-drenched city like LA. Their hair, almost an identical shade of oak-brown, was impeccably groomed: his in an oily combover, hers in shiny victory rolls. A thousand tiny needles prickled Rex's skin as he couldn't shake the feeling he was like a cow, corralled towards the abattoir.

"Mr. Horne," said Bernard, grabbing his hand and shaking it vigorously. "It is an absolute pleasure to meet you."

Betty offered a smile. "We followed the Cinderella case very closely. I actually knew who the killer was all along."

They all did. It still ground Rex's gears every time some nut approached him on the street; they all spoke about the murder investigation as though it were the biggest film of the year. The court case, the sequel. They all seemed to forget the poor girl was a human being. Rex could only imagine the field day the public would have if they got their hands on the whole truth. But Rex smiled at the woman and nodded, the same as he did for all the other looky-loos.

"Maybe you should be a detective." He smirked, his line so rehearsed he did it out of instinct.

"Maybe I missed my calling," said Betty with a cutesy eye roll, then her face dropped. "But then again, it won't take a world-class detective to figure out what happened here."

"Betty," Bernard's voice went down an octave. "Mr. Horne, why don't you come inside and sit down?"

Rex took his place in the cluttered penthouse living room, in a boulder-hard armchair in the corner beside the grand piano. The Aldridges followed behind him like a pair of Siamese twins in a freak show. They were still young; there was plenty of time. Perhaps they were newly married, and the resentment hadn't set in yet.

The droning chatter of car horns and engine roars drifted through the open window from Wilshire, the occasional indiscernible shout.

Betty stared off into the distance with a smile. "Don't you just love the sound of the city? It's like nature's symphony."

An odd thing to say about a man-made concrete jungle. People in *the business* seemed to think offering their unsolicited opinion was a public service, even if they didn't have half a clue what they were yammering on about.

"Sounds like a whole lot of noise to me," Rex laughed it off.

Bernard shrugged. "Well, we're composers. I guess we just see things in a different light."

"Is that how you two met? Composing?"

Betty shot Bernard a sideways glance. She placed a hand over her lips and giggled like a child. Bernard smirked at her, then turned to the detective.

"We get that a lot," said Bernard.

"We're actually brother and sister." Betty hooked her arm into her brother's, the smile wiped from her face. "I don't understand why people find it so hard to comprehend that we live together."

Rex was losing them. He needed to smooth things over. It seemed like Betty braced herself to launch from the sofa, grab him by the ear and march him out of their cluttered penthouse.

Rex held up his hands in surrender. "My apologies. I didn't mean anything by it."

"Not at all." Bernard turned to Betty and placed a hand over hers. "We'll answer any questions you have."

The way the brother stroked his thumb over his sister's index finger sent a cold shiver up Rex's spine. Betty knew something about the case or at least thought she did, and her brother seemed to go to great lengths to keep her quiet.

"I was looking to track down Caroline Lake," said Rex. "I know she is probably lying low after everything that happened with the movie."

Bernard shook his head and rolled his eyes. Rex turned to the brother composer.

"I'm sorry, did I say something wrong?"

Bernard sighed. "It's not you. It's this whole thing. Betty and I went without sleep for weeks to make sure the *Bloomer Girl* - soundtrack was the best version anybody ever heard, but nobody ever talks about that. All they talk about is how Caroline couldn't sing."

Betty shook her head. "Poor Caroline. Then again, I know this is terrible to say, but she did bring it on herself."

"Betty," Bernard whispered.

"You think she shouldn't have taken the role if she couldn't sing?"

"I couldn't give a damn about the movie. I'm talking about her personal life. You and I know better than anyone that Caroline was—"

"Enough!" her brother barked.

"Bernard, she is my best friend. We've known her since forever." Betty turned to Rex. "We used to joke that she was family because she dated Bernard."

"A long time ago," Bernard interjected with a nervous titter. "Years ago. It's not like that makes me a suspect or anything."

"I never said it did," said Rex.

Rex smiled at the man but made a mental note of the tension in Bernard's face. Innocent men didn't fidget about like jittery gerbils. Bernard had the potential for a motive in jealousy that his hard work was ignored in favor of Miss Lake's caterwauling, but it seemed like a stretch for murder. Still, the odd siblings had to believe Rex was in their corner, so he sat back. A few moments of silence and a nervous nelly like Bernard would crack easier than an eggshell.

"The point is, I loved Caroline with all my heart, but it was well known that she made some terrible choices."

Rex's mind sparked with the possibilities—gambling, drugs, alcohol addiction. Which was it? Betty sat her hands in her lap and flattened the seam of her pencil skirt.

"She hung around with *that man*." Betty's voice pinched into a high squeak, and she wiped tears from her eyes with her index finger. "She bought his whole shtick, but I could see through him. People like him only have themselves on their minds."

"You mean colored people?" asked Rex.

Betty's jaw opened, and she stared at Rex. For a moment, he thought she might fly into a rage about his accusations. Instead, she shook her head at him.

"I see you're one of those new-age types." The word came out thick and bitter like oil. "I know it isn't *the right thing to say* anymore, but they aren't like us. They're dangerous."

"Betty," Bernard softened his voice. "You can't go around saying things like that."

"I'm not hearing you say it isn't true."

Tension thickened the already stifling air as Betty stood up and rifled through the hallstand by the entranceway. She returned with some newspaper clippings from the Texarkana Gazette. Photos of teens splattered the front pages.

"This animal had been skulking around shooting teenagers in Arkansas. The first kids were attacked in their car. They were the only two to survive these attacks, and the woman identified the killer as one of them."

Rex had read the articles that trickled out since the first incident in January. The nineteen-year-old woman, Mary Jeanne Larey, did identify the man as sounding black, but she said the man wore a mask. Police believed the woman may have been mistaken, later corroborated by her boyfriend, the only other person to encounter the killer and live to tell the tale. Judging the deep scowl set into young Betty Aldridge's face, she had already firmly cemented her beliefs, and no amount of facts were going to change that.

Chapter 8

Betty yanked a handkerchief from her sleeve and dabbed her eyes. The young woman was a powder keg. One moment laughing with her brother, the next wailing over the suspected death of her best friend. The only real question: was the woman mentally volatile? Or was she a manipulative liar that would stop at nothing to get her way? The former seemed the most likely scenario, but after a decade in the City of Angels, Rex had learned nothing was certain.

"I hope to God I'm wrong about this." Betty crumpled her soggy handkerchief in her fist. "I hope Caroline just ran away with *that man*, and they can ride off into the sunset."

"And that's probably what happened," said Bernard.

The woman's brother took her hand, but she snatched it back and shuffled down the sofa from him. Trouble in sibling paradise. Rex sat in the stone-hard armchair as the scene unfolded. When the cracks showed, the truth usually spilled out.

Betty shot her brother a sneer. "I don't have the luxury of blinding myself to the truth. Even those boobs at the LAPD laughed me out of the room. They didn't even file a report. Probably didn't want to get off their fat butts and do their jobs."

The woman's lips trembled as they sucked in on themselves, cutting deep scowl lines along her cheeks like a ventriloquist dummy.

"Mark my words. She will turn up dead in some back alley in Hyde Park. Of course, it'll be too late for Caroline, if it isn't already."

"Come on now, Betty," Bernard tilted his head, a condescending frown on his face like he was speaking to a child. Even Rex wanted to punch him on the woman's behalf. "Don't you think that sounds a little melodramatic?"

"No, Bernie, it's realistic. Caroline was too good. And now she's paid the price. Why? Because she always saw the good in people."

Rex cleared his throat; better that than a sarcastic scoff. Caroline Lake might have seen the good in others, but Rex couldn't track down a single person beyond Betty Aldridge that could scrounge a kind word about her, and the crazy dame hardly seemed a reliable character witness. Rants and racial prejudices aside, any crumbs on the runaway lovebirds might have yielded some much-needed connections to piece the story together.

"Did you ever meet Mr. Bailey, Miss Aldridge?" asked Rex.

"No," said Bernard, a little too quickly. "*I* saw it, but Betty wasn't there."

While Bernard was quick to answer on his sister's behalf, it had to be true. Miss Aldridge seemed unlikely to stay around when Mr. Bailey was on set.

"So why are you so sure Mr. Bailey did it?" Rex cleared his throat. There was no delicate way to phrase the next part. "Other than his skin color, I mean."

As expected, Betty Aldridge tightened her face into a grimace, her clipped words spitting like bullets.

"There is plenty more, for your information, Mr. Horne. There was the altercation with that saint, poor Mr. Evans."

"At the Neptune Club." Rex nodded. "I heard about that one."

"You mean it happened more than once!" Betty's voice rose to a shrill squeak. "How is this animal not locked up behind bars."

Rex held up a hand. "Wait. What do you mean more than once?"

"We don't know about a fight at any club," said Betty. "But Mr. Bailey came to the set one day. I heard he had been drinking. He roughed up Mr. Evans and shouted at Mrs. Bailey. He called her a whore or something and threatened to kill her."

Bernard shook his head. "That's not exactly what happened, Betty."

"When was this?" asked Rex.

"The last week of shooting," said Bernard. "He barrelled onto the set, screaming in Mr. Evans' face that Billie was his wife, and if Mr. Evans so much as looked at her again, he would come back and slit the crooner's throat."

"Did Mr. Evans say or do anything to him beforehand?" asked Rex.

Bernard shook his head. "Completely unprovoked, far as I could see."

Rex pulled out his flipbook and doodled notes in the maze of clues he'd scribbled in the margins.

"Do you know the car's make and model?"

"It was a beat-up 1926 Chrysler Imperial, jet black with a big gouge running down the passenger door. You can't miss it."

After the Cinderella case, Rex swore to play devil's advocate to understand others' motives. People were inherently good; poor choices were more believable than mustache-twirling villains. But empathizing with Carl Bailey was easier said than done. An insecure man lashing out for fear his wife would get a better offer. It was hardly a new story, but there had to be parts missing; it all seemed too clear-cut.

Maybe Mr. Evans' Jesus freak routine was a grift to lower men's guard so he could swoop in on their wives, the consummate confidence man. It would explain why the crooner was still hanging around a mid-level lounge below his paygrade, even after his and Mrs. Bailey's movie was released to the public.

"Mr. Evans seemed to come out relatively unscathed," said Rex.

"Mr. Bailey got in one good jab to the jaw before our director held him down until security kicked him off the lot."

"James always was a good man," said Betty. "He was willing to do the right thing, even if he had to get his hands dirty."

Did his moral code extend to murdering Mr. Bailey? That didn't explain Caroline's absence. It seemed unlikely the whole thing was a honey trap to lure the man to his death; there were far less convoluted ways to kill a man in Los Angeles, with fewer loose ends.

Rex pulled the wrinkled paper from his pocket and checked the short list of names written in Jimmy Evans' impeccable penmanship.

"James?" Rex found the name in his scribbles. "That's James A. Anthony?"

"Yes." Betty nodded. "Poor James, it must be hard to have people hate you?"

"For kicking a violent man off the set. Hardly seems like reason to hate him."

"Reason enough for Caroline," said Bernard. "She stormed back to her trailer and didn't come out. Halted production for the rest of the day."

Bernard's slightly bloodshot eyes darted between his sister and Rex. The man seemed to grow a few shades paler, if that was even possible.

"But Mr. Bailey assaulted her co-star."

Bernard Aldridge scoffed so loud it came out as a snort. He shook his head as his freckled cheeks turned pink.

"You clearly never met Caroline before."

"She is very particular about things, that's all."

"Betty, let's call a spade a spade. Caroline Lake doesn't care about anyone but herself. You're sitting here, worrying yourself into a state, and I would bet, dollars to donuts, that she is off somewhere with Mr. Bailey, sipping a gin rickey, without even a second's thought for you."

Betty picked at her fingernails, getting more aggressive as she focused. "Caroline would never do that to me. She is my best friend."

"Stop that," said Bernard. "It's rude in front of company."

"Shut up, Bernie!" Betty screamed. "You don't know everything. You don't know what's rude, and you don't know what you're talking about with Caroline. She might fool around with *those men*, but she isn't cruel like them."

Bernard wrapped his arms around his fidgeting sister and hushed her as she mumbled into his shoulder. He stroked a delicate hand through her silky hair, and a chill tingled down the detective's spine.

"I understand," he whispered in her ear, glancing at Rex for a split second. "I know it hurts that Caroline betrayed us. She betrayed us all. And she will probably leave and never see any of us ever again, and we need to accept that. She's happy on a sandy-white beach somewhere."

Betty wailed into her brother's shoulder, and Rex shifted in his seat. Should he get up and leave to give the two a moment alone. Not a sentence he thought he would have to contemplate about a brother and sister.

"I just miss her so much."

Bernard gripped his sister by the shoulders, pulled back, and inspected her puffy eyes. He wiped a tear away with his thumb and offered a smile, which Betty seemed to mimic, but it didn't last long.

"I think I'm feeling a bit of a sore throat coming on," Bernard rubbed his Adam's apple. "Would you be a dear and put on a pot of tea for me?"

"Of course," Betty wiped a tear from her eye and stood up with a smile, straightening her already perfect pencil skirt before she left, sliding the wooden door along the far right wall. Beyond the crowded palace living area was an even more decadent dining room, brightly lit from the city views through the windows. The redwood table in the center hadn't been used for a meal in some time; more a dumping ground for old documents.

Betty pottered out into the kitchen, which was presumably just out of view, as the never-ending apartment seemed to grow like a living, breathing entity. Bernard shot from the sofa and slid the doors closed behind her.

"I'm sorry about Betty, you know, all the black stuff." Bernard rolled his eyes with a wince. "You'd think she stepped right out of the 1860s."

A depleted chuckle ratcheted in Bernard's throat. The man's smile withered like a dead worm, drying out in the sun. He dropped back into his spot on the sofa, head rested in his hands. The young man massaged his scalp with his fingertips, then slowly progressed to his shoulders.

"It gets exhausting explaining this to people all the time. You have no idea what it's like looking after her."

Rex leaned closer as the man lowered his voice, eyeing the sliding door.

"We grew up in Cincinnati," Bernard explained. "Betty was so much happier back in those days; you wouldn't even recognize her back then. She was the most popular girl in school, got the best grades, and even volunteered at the local church every weekend. If I hadn't seen it myself, I wouldn't have believed me."

It seemed a stretch to picture a starry-eyed Betty Aldridge with her hair pinned back, clutching her books with a wholesome smile pressed on her face. But after everything Rex had seen the city do to people, nothing seemed out of the realm of possibility.

"So, what happened to her?"

Bernard focused on the floor and cleared his throat. He opened his mouth, then closed it again before he breathed deep through his nose and continued.

"One day, Betty was volunteering for the church. They sent her to the other side of town to deliver meals to this man. A colored guy that the church looked after." Bernard paused. "She never told us what happened that day, but she came home with a cut lip and a torn dress. You're the detective. I'm sure you can figure it out."

"So now every black man she sees is *him*." Rex shook his head.

"I know it doesn't make what she says okay, but hopefully, you can understand that she isn't a well woman, but she isn't a spiteful person either. Maybe something did happen to Caroline, or maybe she just ran off. Either way, my sister doesn't deserve to go through that. She needs to picture her friend on a beach having fun."

Rex nodded, the words percolating like his morning coffee, stimulating his brain. While he could empathize with the horrors Betty had been through, it seemed like Bernard was going to great lengths to explain them away. Was it that deep down he believed the vitriol his sister spewed, but wanted to appear more liberal in public circles? Or perhaps he was the devoted brother, blind to her blanket hate against the colored man.

The wooden doors slid open, and Betty stood in the doorway with a tray of steaming mugs.

"What're you two talking about in here? Not me, I hope."

Her pink lips slanted to one side as she smirked at them, as though her earlier outburst never happened. Her smile sunk with every passing second, yet Bernard went silent and dipped his head, a waxy sheen glistening over his cream-white skin. His tell was painfully obvious, a flaw that might come in handy if Rex needed to grill him later on. Did that little worm really leave Rex to answer his sister?

"Of course we're not talking about you," Rex chuckled.

His smile pulled against his cheeks so tight they stung, but if he was laying it on too thick, Betty didn't seem to notice.

"So, what were you talking about, then?"

Rex took a sip from his mug. He slurped down the bitter muck, then shot the woman a smile. No reason why the detective couldn't turn this ruse around to suit himself. Hardly seemed like Bernard would object as he stared at his shoes as though he had just discovered the New World.

"We were just talking about the director, Mr. Anthony. I tried to call him, but his office girl said that he was out, and she didn't know when he was coming back. You wouldn't happen to know where I could find him?"

She placed a cup and saucer in front of him. Her blue eyes scanned Rex from his homburg hat to his wingtip shoes and back to his eyes.

"What do you want to speak with him for?" she asked. "You can't think he is a suspect."

"Do I have any reason to think he is a suspect?"

"No," said Betty. "But he seems to be a target for people who can't handle the truth about this country."

"I see." Rex glanced to Bernard, who offered an apologetic wince. "But Ms. Aldridge, I need you to understand I am not looking at Mr. Anthony as a suspect, but I need to get as much information as I can."

The woman eyed him, and Rex turned to Bernard. Something about her stare seemed unhinged, and why wouldn't she be after the horrors that remain in her head.

"Very well," she said, pinching her lips shut. "If James isn't in his office, there's only one place he will be."

Chapter 9

Rex parked before a pair of gaudy gold gates, twisted into ornate flourishes and framed by a stucco-rendered archway. The cursive sign for the Westminster Country Club protruded eight inches from the wall, a slick sheen glistening over the polished brass.

Inside, Rolls Royces and Bentleys glided down the stone pathway cut through the manicured lawn. Rex had been more than pleased with his shiny new Pontiac, but what seconds ago felt like driving on a cloud was now as cumbersome as piloting a Warhawk.

He buried the shame in his chest. Did spending more than most people's homes on some gas-guzzling monstrosity really make them better people?

Rex tightened his grip on the steering wheel and clenched his jaw. A question best left untouched.

He inched the Pontiac towards the hedge-covered stall by the gate. A floral scent with sweet hints of peaches drifted into the car; if only the attendant inside could look half as fresh. The skeletal old coot in the stall hunched over inside the box, his slicked-back hair so thin it looked as though somebody painted the sparse strands with a fine brush.

"Sir, this club is membership only."

The words buzzed in Rex's ears like a passing bee as a black shape appeared in the rear-view. Across the street sat a dive bar that broke the country club's illusion of a Tuscan getaway. Parked out front, a beat-up Chevy puttered by the sidewalk. Rex squinted at the shuddering glass, unable to make out details through the vibrating rear-view. Was it the car Bernard had mentioned? How many busted-up Chevy's could there be in Brentwood?

"Excuse me, sir," said the decrepit attendant. "I said this is members only."

"What makes you think I'm not a member?" asked Rex.

The shaking geezer, who looked as though he might drop dead at any moment of a heart attack or stroke, lowered his head to inspect Rex's mint-green car. He lifted his cloudy eyes with a smile, much warmer than Rex would've thought the wrinkle butler capable.

"Call it a hunch," he said, his voice thin and raspy. "And you didn't click your fingers at me and point at the gate."

"People really do that?" asked Rex, his voice a little distant as he returned to the rear-view. The old clanker was gone.

"Trust me, kid. It's a compliment you don't fit in with these snakes."

Rex bit the inside of his cheek as he tapered his laugh to a smirk.

"Sorry, kid," said the man. "The only way you're getting in is with a guest pass. You know any of these vipers?"

"Well, as it just so happens, I do." Rex pulled a card from his pocket. "I have a pass from Mr. Bernard Aldridge."

Rex handed the man the pass made from thick cardstock, Bernard's details embossed with gold letters. An oily feeling sunk in the detective's gut as he imagined how much it cost to print gilded guest passes, most of which probably went unused. It didn't bode well for Mr. Anthony's character profile; being a director was another strike. The attendant glanced at the card for a split second then handed it back.

"Good enough for me," said the man and pressed a button inside.

The gold gates pulled open with a clank and a mechanical hum. Rex drove down the long driveway, past a hundred yards of green lawns and pompous men in white sweaters playing golf in sandy ditches.

A large peach-colored building with a terracotta tiled roof rolled over the hills. Complete with concrete pillars and a hedge-lined driveway, the stately mansion sprawled one hundred square feet across the estate like a walrus too fat to sit up. Snobs infested the wrap-around porch that seemed more suited to a Kentucky plantation. As Rex pulled up, the women gossiped as they sipped their champagne cocktails while the men boasted, slapping each other on the back as they puffed their Cuban cigars.

It would've been so much easier to hate the Hollywood snobs, but as he stepped out of the car, the appeal of The Westminster Club blossomed before him like a slowly blooming orchid. He breathed in the air, which somehow felt crisper, like they had shipped the oxygen in from a glacier in Norway. So decadent. It forced the detective to savor every moment. Getting the million-dollar treatment without spending a nickel didn't hurt either.

Rex expected the country club to be a damp mansion filled with the stink of dust and decay. Instead, flowers loaded the foyer amongst white marble statues of semi-naked men and women. The room smelled like a fresh garden with the slightest undertones of vanilla.

"May I help you, sir," a voice asked.

An impeccably dressed young man in his twenties smiled at Rex as he jerked back. The detective grabbed his chest and caught his breath for a second. The kid held his hands up in apology.

"I'm sorry to startle you, sir. I was just wondering if I could help you with anything."

The young attendant seemed far from sincere in his attitude, but Rex would take it over the smug little bastard at the Cordelia.

"I, uh," Rex straightened up as he tried to grab his last shreds of dignity off the floor. "I was looking for Mr. Anthony."

"Of course," the man beamed. "Mr. Anthony went out to the golf course about twenty minutes ago. I can take you there now if you so please, but first, we have to get you out of those clothes."

"I beg your pardon." Rex clutched his cotton jacket.

"To play golf," the attendant chuckled. "You can't go out on the green without acceptable attire. We have rentals free of charge in the sporting store out the back. Let me take you."

"Four!" James A. Anthony hollered as he swung his golf club.

The man missed and almost stumbled flat on his backside as he overcompensated with his swing, undercutting the club's persona of golden sun and chirping finches. He bared his teeth and growled, pounding his club into the ground. The caddy, a black kid of no more than fourteen, mumbled an inaudible response.

"It's this four wood," the director shouted. "The damn thing is worthless as a plug nickel."

"Maybe you should swap to a nine-iron." offered Rex. "Might be better for such a close shot."

The man turned to Rex, a face of thunder like the detective just disrespected his mother. He seemed appalled at the notion that somebody would have the guts to question the great James A. Anthony about the sport of golf. Rex had to bite his tongue. The man had to be on either his first or second game in his life, or perhaps James A. Anthony was the most uncoordinated man in history.

The balding man let out a long sigh and readjusted the short red hair that prickled from his temples, with a thick pomade that reeked of axel grease. His fatty chin and balding head made the man look like an egg in a suit.

He stood in an identical white wool sweater, even though it seemed far too warm for either of them—beads of sweat collected on Mr. Anthony's forehead. He pulled a handkerchief from his pocket, dabbing his forehead until he froze on the spot, an all too familiar look of recognition spread across his face.

"I know you," said the director.

Get in line, Rex thought, fighting the urge to roll his eyes.

"Rex Horne." He nodded. "The Cinderella case. Now I just wanted to ask you a few questions about Carl Bailey."

Rex expected the man to explode; if he burst into violence over a placid game like golf, inquiring about the absent Mr. Bailey seemed like a loaded question for the director. But he leaned on his golf club with a smile as though he was ready for an interview about his latest picture.

"What did you want to know?" he asked.

A calm smile rested on the man's face—fishy calm.

"There was an altercation just before you wrapped on *Bloomer Girl*."

"An altercation seems a bit dramatic, don't you think?" The tubby man chuckled so hard it made his whole body wobble. "You sure you aren't an actor."

"What would you call it then?"

"The guy was letting off steam. Everyone's gotta do it now and then."

Rex paused, soaking in the logic. "But he punched a man in the face."

"Come on," Mr. Anthony tilted his head with a furrowed brow. "You can't hold that against him. I'm guessing you've met Mr. Evans already. Don't tell me that whole pious schtick didn't make you wanna sock him one. Besides, a glass of water and a cold steak on the eye, and he came good. No cross, no crown, right?"

The whole persona was nothing like Betty Aldridge's picture of a proud racist who used the attack to get the colored man off his set for good. Either there was more to the story, or Mr. Anthony was trying to cover his tracks.

"So, you don't have a problem with him?"

"Problem?" Mr. Anthony chuckled. "Why would I have a problem with Carl? I spend every other weekend at The Neptune Club."

The director was so convincing Rex almost felt ridiculous to follow up.

"Betty Aldridge said—"

"Say no more," the director shook his head and glanced to his caddy for a moment before returning to Rex. "That woman was relentless, obsessed with Carl Bailey. She was always asking him. Where would he be? When was he coming onto the set? If I didn't know any better, I would've sworn she had a thing for the man."

Mr. Anthony portrayed the young Betty Aldridge as a sexual maniac. Her brother saw her as a shellshocked victim. As somebody who knew the sting of waking in a cold sweat from flashbacks to The Great War, not to mention the horrors of a few years ago, Rex knew a tortured soul when he saw one.

A bitter look must've rested on his face because the director threw his hands up at the detective.

"I'm not saying she was into..." He paused. "*That.* We all know that particular *faux pa* went to Miss Lake."

"Faux pa?" Rex asked.

The remark seemed wrapped in thorny roses. His tone conveyed that the woman used the wrong fork at a country club function.

"Say," Mr. Anthony snapped his fingers at his caddy, then pulled a one-dollar bill from his pocket. "Why don't you get yourself a malt?"

The old man wasn't lying, Rex lowered his gaze.

"For me?" the young boy asked timidly. "Thank you, Mr. Anthony."

The director waited until his caddy was out of earshot.

"I am no different to you or any other man, Mr. Horne. I spend more money than anyone at The Neptune Club. I have no issues with Mr. Bailey or his wife. Hell, Billie wouldn't have been in the picture if I didn't introduce her to the cast."

He said that as though it was a good thing. Rex was yet to see anything beneficial for the lounge singer.

"Mr. and Mrs. Bailey are some of my closest friends." His face drooped, his chubby cheeks hanging over his jawline. "It was Miss Lake with whom I had the problem. She would parade around the studio as though she owned it, never turn up to the sessions on her call sheet, and went outside the boundaries of what nature intended."

"And that was her faux pa?" asked Rex. "Bedding a black man?"

"I think that Mr. Bailey has a place, as do we all, and it is at home with his wife. That's all I'm saying."

The man's face set into a scowl as he seemed to picture the missing actress, no doubt in the arms of Mr. Bailey. Miss Lake's attitude was hardly an isolated incident in Hollywood. As a director, he would've known how to work with difficult people, but her going after Mr. Bailey seemed like the point of no return for the director. He had his heart sent on keeping Mr. and Mrs. Bailey together, and it had nothing to do with his friendship with the couple or the sanctity of marriage.

Chapter 10

Rex shifted on the padded leather bench inside the empty locker room. Wrapped in only a towel, the detective's thick golf pants and itchy sweater lay crumpled beside him. The detective massaged his knees, which screamed at him with sharp stabs from trekking across the spongy golf course lawns. The piano tinkling through muffled speakers to the tune of Ella Fitzgerald's *Into Each Life Some Rain Must Fall* seemed at odds with the damp musk that blanketed the room.

Not that he cared.

If he had to spend one more moment trying to break down Mr. Anthony's angle, he might just hurl his fist through the lacquered rosewood locker behind him. Any distractions were welcome.

Still, some of Mr. Anthony's story seemed on the level; perhaps he was friends with the Bailey's, and his prejudices were misinterpreted by Betty Aldridge. But there was too much that seemed a little convenient, like the fact that the missing couple disappeared after they embarked on an interracial relationship together, a point Mr. Anthony was only too happy to deride. The case was like an iceberg, and Rex had only chipped at the first few inches.

Rex held in a breath as he grunted to his feet and swung his fancy locker open. He placed the items onto the bench when he noticed a white slip of paper between them. He unfolded the document: a flyer for *Bloomer Girl*. Miss Lake's perfectly symmetrical dark features stared wistfully into the distance as though she was yearning for something just beyond her reach. Her red lips were curved into a less-than-inviting smile as red words splattered over the page like they were written with a closed fist grip.

BAK OFF OR ILL KILL YOU

Poorly educated? Or made to appear that way?

A dull thump came from around the corner, and it dawned on Rex that he wasn't alone. The blackmailer might have been still in the room with him; if he was a country club member, Mr. Anthony would shoot to the top of his list.

Rex hobbled around the corner, clutching his towel. He inspected the young man in the next bay of lockers. The young buck he had never met before stared at him, but there wasn't any malicious intent in his eyes; and if he knew who Rex was, he did an excellent job of hiding it.

"Can I help you, buddy?" he said, dropping his eyes. "Because this isn't that kind of locker room."

Heat flushed Rex's cheeks. "No, I just. Somebody left me a threatening letter in my locker, and I thought." Rex turned his back on the man. *Walk away.* "You know what, it doesn't matter."

"Whatever you say, pal," the young murmured.

Rex wanted to crawl into a hole and die after the awkward encounter, but after the threatening letter, he feared Miss Lake may have done just that.

Rex stood in the foyer, breathing in what may be his last chance to sniff the crisp air. The place would be heaven if it weren't crawling with elitists. The sobering thought was enough to push Rex from the building and give his ticket back to the vallet. The kid rushed off the find it, and Rex stood at the end of the stone driveway, watching over the unnaturally green lawns. He managed a couple of serene seconds before somebody tapped him on the shoulder. Expecting the vallet, Rex jumped as a blonde woman in a tweed suit jumped out at him, her hair in unflattering curls with a nose like a condor's beak. She bared her crooked teeth in a devilish grin. "Mr. Horne?" she asked in a thick cockney accent. "I would know that grumpy mug anywhere."

"Sorry, do I know you?" A question Rex asked too much recently.

"How rude of me." The woman reached out a hand, which Rex shook. "Polly Whittingham, editor of The Hollywood Scoop."

"I see." Rex snatched his hand back. "I am more than familiar with your work at The Hollywood Scoop, Miss Whittingham. I read the pieces you wrote about the Cinderella case. For future reference, *neighbor* doesn't have a *U* in it."

The woman offered a smirk. "It does where I come from, love."

Rex clenched his jaw. Nothing would give him more pleasure than to send her back to the Charles Dickens novel she crawled out of.

"And did the mother tongue teach you that there's only one *S-* in *hasn't?*"

"Typos are inevitable, sweetheart. I don't care as much about doing my writing pretty as I do filling it with meaty facts."

The woman said the final word like she had a clue about journalistic integrity. As though the woman hadn't published an article during the Cinderella court case implicating him in the murder, citing the reason as Rex's *desperate need to vie for the adoration of the public.*

"I have nothing to say to you, Miss Whittingham."

"Come on," the woman flashed her crooked teeth. "You can't possibly still be angry about that article. People wanted a bit of excitement in an otherwise dull case, and I gave it to them."

Rex checked his watch and glanced over his shoulder for the vallet, anything to avoid the broad's intense glare.

"What about your latest dramatic episode? That's gotta be interesting?"

Rex brushed a finger over his left pocket. The folded flyer crinkled gently inside, but there was no reason Polly Whittingham would deliver a threat like that unless it was to unsettle him into spilling the beans. Then the British viper could run some poorly cobbled hatchet job on him that he killed Caroline Lake because he wanted to be in the movies.

Seemed almost crazy enough to fit the dame's logic.

Rex cleared his throat. "Miss Whittingham. I have no information about Miss Lake, and even if I did, I wouldn't be sharing it with some hackneyed version of Hildy Johnson."

"I'm a little shocked at you, Mr. Horne." Polly stepped back, a hand on her chest. "You've been working on finding Caroline Lake, and you didn't think to tell us. I remember a time when you used to do a little detective work for us."

"Don't remind me," Rex mumbled.

"So Caroline Lake." Miss Whittingham smirked. "She isn't just in hiding then. Did something happen to her?"

"But you said—" Rex faded out.

"I was going to talk about you and Virginia Lancaster, but this is much juicier."

Rex turned his back to the woman as his heart pounded, shooting a razor-sharp electrical pang through his veins, prickling all the way to his fingertips, which he balled into a fist. The woman's inquiring gaze burned into the back of his head, but he refused to turn around.

He had hung himself once already.

"Come on, Mr. Horne." Her voice grated on his ears. "You know you can trust me."

"Trust you." Rex's cheeks flushed, and he spun around and leaned two feet from the woman's face. "Why don't you leave and do some actual journalism? Go find a story instead of inventing one about me."

"But where's the fun in that?" Miss Whittingham smirked with a shrug.

Rex tightened his lips into a grimace and balled his fist. Bitter words rose in his throat, nasty thoughts he was likely to regret.

"Sir," said the young vallet. "Your car is ready."

Rex snatched the keys back, his eyes never dropping from the alleged journalist. "Thank you."

Rex had buried himself in the case, but he had more pressing issues. He couldn't believe it only took one fight between him and Virginia for her to blab to some friend who would tell Polly Whittingham, and the last thing the blonde shark needed was any more ammunition. He got in his Pontiac and slammed the door.

It was time the pair had words.

"Grovelling back?" asked Virginia.

The actress leaned against the doorframe to her Spanish-style castle in a simple powder-blue silk nightgown. She took a seductive drag of her cigarette, then puffed silver smoke onto the afternoon air. "About time, too. I was started to get bored of this little game."

After she belittled his experience in the war, then spat all over the memory of his dead comrade, she guarded the door like a waifish soldier. As though she deserved an apology. Just so Rex could have the privilege to step inside and give her the business.

"Where the hell do you get off, missy?" Rex's voice dropped.

"Missy?" Virginia scoffed. "What am I, six years old? You're not my father, darling. You couldn't hold a candle to that man. He would never have spoken to me the way you have."

"Maybe because you haven't blabbed his business to everybody in the Hollywood Hills."

"What are you blathering on about now?" Virginia rolled her eyes. "Because if this is your not so clever way of trying to change the subject, then—"

"After everything we went through last night, you haven't learned a thing about the disrespect you showed me."

"Disrespect?" Virginia giggled.

"Yeah," Rex lowered his voice. "You're out airing our dirty laundry across Los Angeles. I had Polly Whittingham track me down and ask about you and me."

Virginia's face dropped. "You didn't tell her anything."

Rex stood silent.

"Why would I do a foolish thing like that?" Virginia screamed. "Polly Whittingham is the most venomous reporter in all of Los Angeles. She'd sell her own mother out for a front-page story. She didn't give any details, did she?"

"No," Rex lowered his gaze.

"You really are a twit sometimes." Virginia shrugged. "She was fishing."

The fine creases in Virginia's hands wrinkled as she interlocked her fingers. A ten-pound ball of guilt hung in Rex's chest. He had been wrong on that front and abused her for his walking into a trap. In his hubris, he thought he was the only one that could catch people in a trap. Yet he was so quick to throw Virginia under the bus and take the word of that buck-toothed shark over the woman who shared his bed. It suddenly seemed foolish to underestimate how far a ruthless tabloid journalist would go to get the skinny on a juicy story. All so she could take a pinch of facts and a whole lot of spite and roll it into a half-baked mess of spelling errors and blatant lies.

He opened his mouth, but his jaw hung open for a few seconds as the inevitable apology never arrived. He couldn't lose sight of the actual argument. Virginia sided with Benson, even after Rex told her what a monster the whiny rich kid was.

"I don't have time for this." Rex turned his back and headed for the Pontiac, parked at the top of the steep concrete driveway.

"Oh, no you don't," Virginia's footsteps clicked behind him. "You don't get to walk away from me. So what? You're mad at me. Then let's deal with this."

Rex slumped into the Torpedo's driver seat. Virginia trotted beside the car and grabbed the door before he could slam it shut.

"I won't apologize for wanting to keep you safe," she barked.

"I already told you," said Rex. "Benson is bad news. My word should be enough."

"Well, it's not." Virginia folded her arms, inadvertently pushing up her cleavage just outside Rex's window. Part of Rex wondered if it was a deliberate plot. He had to give her credit. It was working. Still, he stood his ground. If he could abstain from the Fleischmann's, he could do the same with Virginia.

"I like that you worry about me, but I can take care of myself."

Fate was a cruel mistress. As Rex turned the key and the engine fired up, the flyer dropped from his pocket, and Virginia picked it up. The moment she unfolded the wrinkled paper, her eyes widened. Her jaw hung open.

"This is you handling the situation." Virginia crumpled the flyer up and hurled the defaced flyer into the car. "Someone sends you a death threat, and you bury your head in the sand."

"I've got a plan."

"Well, by all means." Virginia tossed her arms in the air, as dramatic as expected for an actress of her caliber. "And what pray tell is this wonderful plan that will stop you from getting killed?"

"Caroline Lake has a place in San Francisco," Rex barked back. "I'm going to drive down there tonight and see if she's there. If she's there, we can put an end to it."

"And what do you think you'll do when you get to San Francisco? Look her up in the Yellow Pages?" Virginia rolled her eyes. "The woman is a celebrity. She isn't going to have a public listing. You want to find her. You might need me to *blab* to one of my actor friends."

"Clever," Rex sneered. "What's the catch?"

Virginia pressed a hand to her chest in mock surprise. "Honestly, I'm a little hurt you think so little of me. I'll find her address. However, I am coming with you."

The inevitable *however*.

She was always unwilling to compromise and told things precisely as she saw them. It was what made her so alluring in the first place, but now her honest silver tongue had undoubtedly lost some of its shine.

"You know I like your honesty, Virginia—"

"Then listen to me." Virginia's voice softened. "I'm sorry that I cannot play the dutiful wife, waiting at home praying that your stalker doesn't catch up with you. That isn't me. So, if you want Caroline's address, I am going to come with you and keep you safe."

Chapter 11

The car rocked as Virginia thumped her third suitcase into the trunk. Rex had killed the engine, and the vehicle was heating like a kiln in the afternoon sun—still, no point emptying the tank while Virginia picked out the perfect pair of shoes. Caroline Lake might've died of old age in the time it took Virginia to organize herself. Rex watched in the rear-view as the actress struggled in a green pinup dress, a red scarf wrapped around her hair, and a pair of sunglasses, so oversized they covered two-thirds of her face. First, there was the makeup, and then her first three outfits were *a little more LA than San Francisco.*

Rex rolled his eyes. Hardly like they were bound for Tokyo for the next three months.

He fought the twinge that tugged in his gut, urging the gentleman in him to help her, but she still hadn't apologized. The deal to take her along was nothing more than extortion.

Virginia slammed the trunk shut, strutted around the car, and slid into the passenger's seat, all while clutching her scarf so as not to ruin her hair. A floral waft of her Chanel No. 5 sent a conflicting jolt through Rex's brain. A familiar flutter dampened by scorching irritation. She shot him a glare, which Rex ignored as he restarted the car and screeched off down the steep driveway.

They drove out of Los Angeles through San Fernando. For hours, they marinaded in awkward silence until they reached Santa Clarita. Virginia stared out the window, not sharing a word. Well, two could play that game, and he wasn't going to be the one to crack. But long seconds passed. Pressure mounted in his brain.

"Don't you think this silent treatment is a little childish?" Rex snapped.

A euphoric wave washed over him as he released the tension, immediately followed by a dense brick in his throat. He played right into her little game. Worse than embarking on an argument, Virginia remained mute, staring out the window at the tidy houses stacked in neat rows. A fight would've been better than the silence. Now Rex was left alone with Caroline Lake in his head for the rest of the trip.

An ethereal fog hung over the Golden Gate Bridge as the Pontiac tore down the Eisenhower Highway over the San Francisco Bay. The bridge's gold lights breaking through the dense fog felt like an omen, as though Caroline Lake's spirit was guiding him towards her body. Of course, Rex didn't hold with that kind of occultist nonsense, but he could shake the jagged concrete cluster in the pit of his stomach that told him they weren't going to find her alive and well in her apartment.

They pulled up outside the massive house at Balboa Terrace. The odd wooden facade mixed with the tiled roof gave the impression of an overfed Bavarian cottage. The swaying ferns and topiaries seemed to be in order. Still, it wasn't out of the realms of possibility that some gardener permanently toiled only for them to stay locked away forever like trapped souls in some witch's garden.

Virginia got out of the car and strode up the stone driveway without a word.

"What are you doing?" Rex growled. "This is trespassing."

"Really?" said Virginia as she picked up her step. "Because I would call it dropping in unannounced on an old friend, which might be considered somewhat uncouth, but far from a crime."

Rex bit the inside of his cheek as they both trekked up the driveway to the wisteria-draped porch. The disgusting purple plants rocked in the chilly evening breeze. They reminded him of the smell of the kitty litter box in his childhood home. He flicked the stinking flowers out of his face as he raced past Virginia and rapped his fist on the varnished door. As expected, nobody answered.

Rex leaned against the window. The living room inside sat perfectly still, like a neglected museum exhibit—Caroline Lake movie posters for films like *Below the Waves* and *Lamentable Souls* lined the terracotta wallpaper. A thick layer of dust collected around the coffee table wedged between two red leather sofas.

"What are you doing here?" asked a female voice.

Virginia squealed, and Rex spun around, almost knocking the little granny behind him to the ground. The white-haired woman clutched her pearl necklace, her milky eyes sparkling with the hint of tears.

"I am so sorry, ma'am," said Rex. "I didn't see you there."

"What are you doing here?" she asked. "I saw you two coming in here, and I thought you were a couple of burglars."

"I am here to see Miss Lake, an old friend." Virginia smiled.

"I've seen you before," said the old woman. "You were in that picture with Miss Lake years ago. *Six Inches Under Phoenix* or something."

"Really?" Virginia smirked, adjusting her hair as though it could move with the number of chemicals she put in it. "Are you a fan?"

The old woman spat over her shoulder. "It was an awful film."

Rex had to fight the smirk stretching across his face. He liked this crotchety old broad.

"Well, I guess there's no accounting for taste." Virginia rolled her eyes.

"I'm afraid you have us at a disadvantage," said Rex. "How did you know Miss Lake?"

"Jean Lockhart. I run the inn next door." She pointed beyond the lawn. "There are still some vacancies if you were interested in staying the night."

"I don't think so," said Virginia, eyeing the woman. "We were just there to see Miss Lake."

"Well, you came for nothing, I'm afraid," said the old lady. "Caroline hasn't shown her face in here since Christmas. It wouldn't surprise me if she never showed her face around here again."

Rex let out an exhausted sigh. He wasn't sure he had the energy to deal with another story about Miss Lake's privileged actress routine.

"I'm sorry, am I boring you?" the old woman grumbled.

"It's hardly an engrossing story."

"Well, it might seem like small news out there in Hollywood, but when she brings a violent criminal into our neighborhood—"

"Violent criminal?" asked Virginia Lancaster.

"A brute of a man," said the old woman. "The LAPD wants him for a list of crimes. It would take me a week to reel them off."

"You're talking about Carl Bailey?"

"The colored man." The old woman nodded.

"And how do you know he was a violent criminal?"

"Because I had a good friend tell me all about it."

"And who might this good friend be?"

"Someone who worked on Caroline's last picture." The old dame beamed as though they were supposed to be impressed. "She was a composer for the film."

Rex ran a finger through his hands. "Betty Aldridge."

"Do you know what, dear?" Virginia linked her arm in his; she was almost convincing, even to him. "Perhaps we should take this charming woman up on her gracious offer. After all, it is getting so late, and I don't think it would be safe for you to drive home in such a state. It might be nice to stay at this charming woman's inn for the night."

Lord knows Virginia packed for it.

Virginia shot him a look that telegraphed her intentions. He could almost hear her husky British voice in his head. *I've got a plan. Don't question me in front of the old cow.* Then, the actress turned back to the broad and smiled.

"You see, we never really had a honeymoon together, and things have been rather tense between us lately, and I'm sure a charming evening at your quaint little getaway. Now come along, dear, and don't forget to grab my bags from the car."

Chapter 12

"This room is positively revolting!" Virginia announced with a volume that could only be intended for the old bat that ran the joint. "I knew we would have to slum it in this dog kennel she calls an inn, but you would expect some quaint charm to it, surely."

"Will you shut up?" Rex grunted from the corner of the stiff mattress. "I think the old broad got the message."

Icy silence.

"Well, I guess that's the honeymoon over then, I suppose."

Virginia's mouth puckered like she had chowed down on a whole bag of lemons, but at least it stopped her hammy performance. She chipped off the flaking paint from the cracked wall by the tiny box window. She scrutinized the grey specs between her fingers, muttering inaudible barbs.

Rex wouldn't confess it, but she was right. The mid-sized house turned inn left a lot to be desired, from the murmurs of other guests that leaked through paper-thin walls to the lack of privacy in their poky broom closet of a room.

Virginia sat on the edge of a dresser and inspected her nails, like a wounded cat grooming itself out of shame.

"So, I suppose this Betty Aldridge is the top suspect in this case?"

"What makes you say that?" asked Rex.

The detective turned his back to her as he slid out of his wingtips. An instant pressure release sent a wave of fresh blood tingling through his body. He closed his eyes with a sigh.

"She seems to have a vendetta against this Mr. Bailey," Virginia soliloquized. "She must've had some kind of altercation?"

"She never met the man," said Rex. "It's a long story, but she has a thing against black men."

"I see," Virginia lowered her head. "I almost hate to bring this up, but there might be an angle you haven't considered."

Virginia sauntered across the room and sat on the stiff bed, her back to him. She still seemed irritated but willing to help him with the case, or perhaps she was simply digging for dirt on Miss Lake.

"You're assuming that if something happened to Caroline, it was a cast or crew member."

"You're point?" Rex shrugged.

"What if you got the wrong end of the story. Have you considered the possibility that Miss Aldridge might be right?"

Rex spun around and narrowed in on the woman. Did he even know her? It wasn't like he considered himself a champion of the colored man, but he had fought alongside black pilots in the war, and he had their backs the same as any other. Virginia's sudden sympathy for the misguided Betty Aldridge had him taken aback.

"You can't really believe that," said Rex.

"Rex, please," said Virginia, but Rex cut her off.

"Because I saw what this kind of thinking does. I watched arbitrary Nazi hate decimate Europe over the last couple of years. *He* thought that colored folks were evil too, you know."

"Will you get down off your high horse," Virginia snapped. "I never once said that. This Betty character sounds like a spiteful cow. But perhaps hearing this from a screwy woman like her has blinded you to the possibility that this man is responsible for doing something to Caroline. Have you spoken to his wife to see if he ever struck her?"

Virginia shrunk like a wilting lily in the harsh sun. She joined her hands, and if Rex didn't know any better, he'd swear she was praying.

"If anybody is going to know the true Carl Bailey, it was his wife."

As Rex glanced at the actress over his shoulder, she turned to him, chewing her lip. She was obviously holding back on something.

"Whatever it is, Virginia, just say it."

"We need to get in Caroline's house."

"Okay, take it down a notch, Nancy Drew," said Rex. "That's breaking and entering."

"I don't know about you," Virginia rooted around her suitcase and pulled out some evening gloves, which she slid over her hand. "But I didn't come all this way to go back with my tail between my legs. I intend to find out more about her relationship with this man."

"You can't go in there."

"You want to protect me." Virginia shot a smirk. "You'll have to come with me."

Virginia punched her gloved fist through the window, which shattered with a sharp crack that echoed into the black night. The two of them froze for a moment as though the police were going to appear and arrest them instantaneously. Nothing happened, not that Rex really believed it would, but instinct made people do some stupid stuff.

Rex interlocked his hands and boosted Virginia through the broken window. She tumbled to the living room floor inside. But Rex wouldn't even consider going through with his knee. That was a recipe for disaster.

"Alright," he whispered. "No, go unlock the back door in the kitchen. I'll meet you there."

Rex skulked around the back of the house to the wooden landing overlooking the grassy lawn. The engraved rosewood door swung open with a click, and Virginia held a flashlight under her chin.

"Well, hello, Mr. Horne?" She lowered her voice so deep it was barely audible. "Come in."

"Very funny," Rex shot the woman a stink eye, then entered the kitchen.

The stench of rotting fruit soaked into the air. As Virginia's flashlight tracked over the room, flashes of checkered floors and rounded pea-green cabinets filled the room.

"Bet you're glad I bought three suitcases now. My younger brother was in the Scouts, and you know their motto. Always be prepared."

"Well," Rex grumbled. "Just keep it away from the windows. Clearly, the busybody next door has nothing better to do but watch an empty house."

Virginia's red lips wilted slightly as she glanced off into the distance, and a twinge of guilt prickled his skin, but he pushed it down with the rest of his feelings and walked past her.

"So where does one even start to search a house this big."

"The bedroom," said Rex.

"Mr. Horne," Virginia's went up an octave. "Does this mean you've forgiven me?"

It was a semi-successful attempt at seduction. It wasn't bad, but not enough to make the detective cave.

Rex turned his back on her. "People keep their most intimate things in their bedrooms."

Rex shuffled to the barely visible marble staircase leading to the second floor. Rex stumbled up the steps, one at a time. Virginia decided to upstage him and practically leaped up the stairs like an Olympic hurdler, but Rex took it one step at a time. How could he explain to the cops if he crippled himself on the steps and had to call them to rescue him like a cat in a tree?

"I found it," Virginia screamed like a child on Christmas morning. "I found the bedroom."

Now at the top of the stairs and thoroughly out of breath, Rex wasn't sure he had the energy to explain the no noise rule again; a fat lot of good it would've done anyway.

Rex stumbled into the darkened bedroom, with only a faint trace of silver moonlight breaking through the crack in the thick curtains and the erratic flashlight beam flailing around the space. Musk seemed to fill the house, as though nobody had inhabited it for months, not even a cleaner.

Textured maroon carpet graced the floors, while ornately decorated blue wallpaper shimmered in the flashlight's glow.

There was no mistaking it as the master bedroom. The bloated room was twice the size of Rex's office, with a custom-built bed that was every bit the size of two kings. Either side of the opulent monstrosity was a relatively small rosewood bedside table, each topped off with a no-doubt costly gold lamp with a frosted glass cover that looked like an unbloomed flower. Rex gestured Virginia to the left and moved over to the right. He pulled out the drawer and rifled through scraps of paper and an old hairbrush.

Hardly a gold mine.

Virginia gasped, then let out a little squeak. "I found something."

"What is it?" asked Rex, sliding the drawer closed.

"They appear to be love letters," said Virginia. "Would it kill you to write me love letters?"

"It might have killed them," said Rex, James A. Anthony's smug face plastered across his brain. "What does it say?"

Virginia cleared her throat and pointed the flashlight at the paper, the yellowish light bouncing off her face as she adjusted her posture as though she was preparing for an audition.

"My darling Caroline," Virginia's voice shifted into a husky whisper. "Every moment I spend with you is pure agony, and I fear I cannot take the pain in my chest any longer. I was lured by the siren's call, fooled by her song, and now she had bared her claws and has them permanently embedded in my soul, never to let go. If I were a better man, a stronger one, I would let you go and let her drown me alone, but I know with your help, I can leave this siren to dry out on the shore, and we can finally be together."

Virginia's face puckered as though she had been served a place of rotting meat. A creepy vibe certainly tinged the note.

"You still want me to write letters like that?"

"I take that back," Virginia's eyes dropped to the letter once more. "I think I would rather my grizzled detective any day of the week than that lying snake."

A sense of personal hostility filled Virginia's voice. As Rex made his way around the three yards of bed, her fingers trembled with the note like a war wife who had just been delivered the news that she was a widow. Rex clasped her cold hands in his.

"What's wrong?" he whispered.

"His molasses sweet words," Virginia plonked onto the edge of the colossal bed. "I've heard them all before."

Virginia stared forward. For a moment, Rex thought she was prompting him to ask for more information, but the more he stared at the crinkled crow's feet in the corner of her eyes, it was clear she was mustering the nerve to tell him something.

"Henry," the word came out thin and clipped. "He was my second husband. He used to have sickly sweet words just like those ones, but they were only to coat the poison inside."

Rex didn't have words to smooth everything over for all his bedside manner as a detective, perhaps because there weren't any. Some scars ran so deep nobody could fix them; they just had to be lived with for the rest of your life. So, he stayed silent. Sometimes the best thing to do was listen.

"Every time he threw me down the stairs or practically wrenched my hair out by the fistful, he would have the sweetest things to say about me. There was always someone or something that caused his erratic outbursts. He apologized profusely and told me that he couldn't live without me. But it was never truly an apology, just sweet words like Mr. Bailey's. And if you listened to his apologies, you wouldn't know the man had a spiteful bone in his body. Everybody thought Henry had the heart of a poet because none of them saw his darker side."

"His true side," said Rex, clenching his teeth as he wanted to track down this Henry and give him the business.

"It was no truer than any other side," said Virginia. "And that was the problem. His sweet side wasn't a facade. It felt just as real as any other, and perhaps that's why I made so many excuses for him."

The profile would undoubtedly fit what little he had seen of the Bailey's, and he had seen enough from his drunken mother in his childhood and the string of men she brought into their home. She was so desperate for affection she put up with a lot. A couple of them smacked her around and Rex, but she would constantly make excuses for them for fear they would leave her alone.

"I'm sorry," said Rex. "This whole thing has been my fault. My stupid pride got in the way. I know we've had our troubles, but I want you to know I would never do that."

"I know," Virginia cupped a hand over his.

A whirring of sirens rang off in the distance.

"We've got to get out of here," said Rex.

He and Virginia bundled the letters and made for the staircase. When they reached the second-floor balcony, they had a good view of the entryway as two uniformed officers rapped on the front door. Rex grabbed Virginia and pulled her back into the bedroom. He pressed a finger to her lips as the officer called to them across the cavernous entryway.

"Anybody in there," said the officer. "If that's you Hartman kids again, you'd better come out now."

Rex and Virginia stifled a giggle as the policeman continued and eventually lost interest.

"This is exciting, isn't it?" she asked, pressing his hand against her chest. "Feel my heart. It's pounding."

The smiles dropped from their faces, and they both leaned in. Warm breath tickled Rex's lips in the drafty mansion. Rex glided his hand down the zipper of her pinup dress as he leaned in to kiss her soft lips.

Chapter 13

"Alright, kids, listen up," the policeman's gruff words climbed up to the second floor.

The cigar ravaged voice echoed off the polished marble, trickling in through the open door to the master bedroom. But the words buzzed in his ears like a mosquito until Virginia pulled away and shot him a smirk, scraping an acrylic nail along the corner of her mouth.

"Did you hear that?" she tittered. "He thinks we're a couple of teenagers."

"We're kind of acting like them," Rex whispered.

Virginia's spell dissolved as she pulled away, and the enormity of his situation hit him like a cinder block. He wasn't a teenager; breaking and entering didn't make him a little scamp. It made him a felon.

"Probably just the Freeman kids again," said a much younger-sounding man. "I've got Lily waiting at home with supper, and you know how she gets when it goes cold."

"You've had your fun," said the gruff officer. "Now come out."

Rex's heart punched against his ribcage as his throat turned to sandpaper. He crept to the edge of the doorway, then snuck out onto the second-floor balcony and peered over. The two uniformed officers inspected the grand entryway in the dark, flash-beams waving around like air-raid searchlights. Rex pushed Brittany's ashen skies and decimated buildings down into his chest. He ignored the grating groan of air raid sirens that clawed against his skull.

He couldn't focus on anything but getting out.

Virginia's green eyes sparkled from the dark like a cat as her fingers curled around the white doorframe. Rex gestured to follow him, and she crouched low and made her way over. Rex took one step down the stairs, and white-hot pain shot up his leg, pinching against every nerve in his body. He clutched the banister with one hand and bit down on the other to stop the low groan begging to come out.

Virginia hooked her arm in his, and Rex breathed the cloud of Chanel No. 5 that followed her. The moment could almost have been considered sweet. Rex felt less like her beau on the red carpet of some premiere and more like an elderly father she helped off the John. Still, he clutched her arm. The goal was getting out. The dilemma of Virginia seeing him as a feeble old geezer would have to wait.

Relief washed over Rex as he lifted his last foot from the stairs and planted it on the first-floor tiles. It was short-lived as the cops, who were now rooting around in the kitchen, went silent. Stifling silence hung over the mansion, which now felt more like a tomb. Rex and Virginia had gone to great lengths to be quieter than mice, but even the craftiest mouse eventually got its neck broken by a trap.

"They obviously went out this way," the younger cop's voice echoed from the kitchen. "The kids will be long gone now."

"You're probably right," said the older cop.

"Can we go home now?"

As the policemen rambled, Rex shuffled towards the front door the police had jimmied open. They both shuffled towards the entrance, but something flashed in the corner of his eye, and Rex stopped. Virginia ran for the front door. Her stilettos cracked like thunder in the cavernous foyer.

"Did you hear something?" the older cop's voice echoed.

"Hurry up, Rex," Virginia whispered. "We have to get out of here."

Rex stared in a daze at the object as his mind tinkered away.

"Do you want to go to jail?" asked Virginia.

A sharp crack rang across his face, and acute pain prickled over his left cheek as it sunk in that Virginia had slapped him.

"I'm sorry," Virginia kept her voice at a husky whisper. "But unless you want to spend the night in a prison cell, we need to leave now."

Rex lay beside Virginia on the stone slab mattress inside the poky broom closet bedroom at the end of the hall. Hours had passed, and they had a reasonably vigorous victory roll between the sheets; as athletic as anybody could get after wearing down the cartilage in their knees running from the cops. Despite this, the detective lay awake, too pepped up on adrenaline to sleep.

Rex revised his waking nightmare with each passing minute, each edition scarier than the last. He expected the police to barge through the door and arrest them for destruction of property, burglary, you name it. Naturally, in the current revision, Benson was the one to book him. As he hauled Rex from the building in handcuffs, a slick grin spread over the man's mouth, exaggerated like a rubber-faced cartoon villain.

The press' flashbulbs blinded him as Benson loaded him into the paddy wagon. The detective's shame surged through the glorified beat cop's body like electricity, charging him like a Tripp Lite battery.

Rex pinched his mouth shut and clenched his fist as his mind replayed the horror show, even darker and more indulgent than the last.

"I'm sorry," said Rex. "I've behaved like a jackass."

"You have," Virginia scoffed, then paused a beat. "But I have been living up to my name of the Bitch of Burbank, huh?"

Rex wasn't about to step into that trap.

"You deserve an explanation," said Rex. "About the whole Benson thing. You see, he wasn't just someone who served under me. His father appointed him as my protege. He was to shadow me. My best friend Max Holloway was against it, but I believed following orders was what good soldiers did. So, I mentored the kid. He never listened to me. He did whatever he wanted, ordering the others around. I did nothing."

Max's wide grin filled Rex's brain. Holloway seemed like the only person who would understand the Benson problem. He chewed his lips and kept going before the yips set in.

"We went out on a rescue mission to save some POWs in Brittany. We had a plan, but in his infinite wisdom, Benson decided he would take point. He goes rogue, and Holloway is shot down and killed. A couple of krauts attack my plane, and a couple of kids who

I think to be Nazis drag me back unconscious to an abandoned apartment building."

"Felix," Virginia whispered the word as though she were mentioning the devil.

"I don't pretend that I had nothing to do with that poor boy's death, but none of it would've happened if that little pipsqueak didn't see everything as a pissing contest."

"I am sorry," Virginia whispered. "Was that why you stopped?"

"What?" asked Rex, rolling over to face her.

"In Caroline's house, at the front door." Virginia shuffled closer. "You froze, and your eyes went all blank. It was almost like you saw a ghost."

"You're not going to go all kooky on me, are you?" Rex joked.

"Stop avoiding my question," she said. "You saw something. What was it?"

Rex's brain had burned the image into his skull since they returned.

"It was the strangest thing," said Rex. "There was a hallstand by the front door, and on it was a photo of Caroline Lake with Carl Bailey."

Virginia knotted her brow as she seemed to struggle to find the point. "But what does that have to do with the price of fish?"

"What?" asked Rex, taken aback by her British slang. He shook the thought from his head and continued. "You had to see them in the picture to understand. For all the publicity still and pictures in the paper, I've never seen Caroline Lake seem as genuinely joyful as she did in this photo."

The image had been seared into Rex's brain since they left Miss Lake's mansion. She laughed, head tilted back, eyes closed. Mr.

Bailey's inky black hands clutched her breast as he nuzzled into the crook of her neck. Rex felt dirty looking at it, as though it was mildly pornographic. Still, somebody had to be there to take the photo, watching this intimate moment.

"It just seems so strange," Rex pontificated. "How could people go from so madly in love with one another to wanting to commit murder?"

"You put too much stock in photos, dear," said Virginia. "Henry and I had scrapbooks jammed packed full of happy photos at elegant galas in beautiful suits and dresses. It didn't change the fact that we were both miserable. The lens doesn't pick up the bruises I slathered with a pound of Covermark."

Rex held Virginia, stroking her supple forearm as he contemplated the options. She was right, there was every chance that Carl Bailey was abusive, but it still seemed just as likely that some racist busybody who couldn't keep their nose out of other people's business took matters into their own hands.

Virginia placed a hand over the detective's heart, circling a finger through the silver chest hair. Rex's chest fluttered.

"Sweetheart, you can't go on like this. You'll drive yourself insane if you don't let it go. I saw a charming little cafe on the way in here. Why don't we go for breakfast tomorrow so you can take your mind off the case?"

The happy couple from the photo still haunted Rex as he sat on the white steel furniture in the outdoor dining area of the Bay View Cafe. The detective shifted his greasy bacon and eggs around the plate. He wasn't pouting; lord knows he'd done a lifetime's worth over the last twenty-four hours. Virginia sipped her coffee mug and gripped it as she stared out over the San Francisco Bay Area, the crisp ocean wind flicking through her dark hair. She ripped apart a few slices of toast and pecked at them like a bird. She shot Rex a pity-soaked smile.

"Look, I know this whole Caroline thing bothers you," she said, popping another piece of shredded toast in her mouth. "But I'm glad that you agreed to this trip, or maybe I should thank myself for extorting my way onto it."

A smile cracked Rex's lips, and Virginia's green eyes glowed.

"That's the grizzled sweetheart I've come to love." She cleared her throat. "Having around here, I mean."

"Well, I love—" Rex mimed clearing his throat "—having you around too."

He shot Virginia a wink and tucked into his overcooked eggs. They ate together in silence, but there was a comfort between them like they were a pair of well-worn shoes. They didn't need to fill the silence. They were just happy in each other's company.

"Starlet feared dead," a kid no older than ten shrieked on the street corner. "Finger found in an abandoned lot."

Rex and Virginia both dropped their knives and forks in unison and stared at each other. They stared for a few beats as Rex tried to assess the situation. Could it be that simple? A kid hocking newspapers made a break in the case.

"You don't suppose—" Virginia stopped, as though she didn't want to jinx their luck. "It couldn't be, right?"

"Hey kid," Rex stood and dug fifteen cents out of his pocket. "I'll have one of those."

Rex tossed the kid three nickels, and he threw back a newspaper, which landed in his breakfast. Not that Rex could eat the overcooked muck when he had the answers he needed right in front of him. Virginia rose from her seat and read the article over his shoulder.

FINGER FOUND, STARLET DEAD?

Growing fears are mounting for actress Caroline Lake after a nearby resident discovered a severed finger in an abandoned lot next door to the Brentwood Theater. According to LAPD officer Chaz Benson, he also found a piece of jewelry near the body. "We are running a cross-check with local jewelers in the Brentwood area. It won't be long before the truth comes out, and then I will bring the maniac behind this senseless violence to justice."

Benson's words were so oily Rex half-expected them to roll off the page. He posed at the crime scene with that same plastic grin. Did he need to hold a gun to anybody's head to get that shot taken?

But that isn't the only thing the suave young detective was up to. "We have been checking the image against any picture we can find, publicity stills, photos from The Hollywood Scoop, but we have come up with nothing yet. Still, it's early days, and we intend to make a break in the case any day now."

Virginia rubbed his shoulders. "I'm sorry, darling. It seems as though you can't escape the little weasel."

"I don't care about him," Rex rose from his seat and took her hand. "Do you realize who lives opposite that abandoned lot?"

Chapter 14

Rex tapped his foot in the phone booth opposite the Brentwood Theater. The receiver rang in his ear as he checked his champagne-faced Rolex. Five-thirty. The Neptune Club opened in a couple of hours. With her husband missing, there was nowhere else Mrs. Bailey could be.

Rex stared at the empty lot through the sweaty phone booth's murky glass. Orange sunset bounced off the pale dirt as a few stray cops bagged the last scraps of evidence.

The phone clunked to life, and a panting voice answered.

"Hello?" puffed Billie's unmistakably smooth voice.

A man murmured down the other end, but after a muffled hush, everything went quiet. Was it crazy to think that the Bailey's were the con artists all along? Perhaps they worked in tandem to trap Miss Lake like a couple of wolves. There was still yet to be a motive. Maybe he needed to check into the actress' financial affairs. She may have been in love in that photo, but for Carl, it could've been a long con.

"Mrs. Bailey," said Rex. "I just wanted to know if you've heard from your husband lately?"

"I haven't heard from Carl since he left me," she said. "But I'm not sure I appreciate the insinuation, Mr. Horne."

"I'm not insinuating anything," said Rex.

Although Rex was pinning suspects for the man on the other end of the phone as she spoke. Perhaps she and Mr. Evans were having that affair her husband worried about, or maybe she was harboring Mr. Bailey since he returned to her after killing Miss Lake. Or, more likely, it was a busboy asking a question at an inopportune moment, and Rex's PI imagination was way out of line.

"I hired you to find my husband. If he were here with me, there would be no point of you."

Rex scribbled notes about the strange man on the other end into his notepad as the woman continued on a tirade about her husband's honor. It seemed peculiar, but people often tried to please those who treated them worst.

Treat 'em mean, keep 'em keen.

"Miss Bailey," said Rex. "I'm sorry if I caused you any insult. I only ask because—"

"I know why you asked," she snapped. "The same reason that cop Benson came sniffing around here. Of course the black man is a violent beast that smacks his wife around. He had to have something to do with that finger turning up in Brentwood, right?"

"Well," Rex stretched the word. There was a chance his next sentence could destroy his shot at a paycheck. "I have heard from multiple sources about an incident with your husband and Mr. Evans that sounded particularly damaging to your husband's reputation."

The line went quiet. Rex slapped the telephone, assuming the connection was dead, then the woman's tinny voice screeched down the other end of the phone.

"Sorry about that. I have no agenda when it comes to your husband. But I would be grateful if you could help me make some sense of this. What can you tell me about the day your husband attacked Mr. Evans?"

"You need to understand something about us," the woman went silent for a moment. "Everything we have, this club, this beautiful life we have built, was the result of hard work. Nobody ever handed anything to us."

"But someone handed it to Mr. Evans?"

"Forget about Jimmy," Mrs. Bailey groaned.

Rex was failing to see the point. What did any of it have to do with Mr. Bailey?

"My husband pulled us both out of Hyde Park and really made a name for us. And there's a certain amount of pressure that comes with that. It makes him highly strung, and he might lash out from time to time, but you don't understand the strain he is under."

Rex took a deep breath, held it, then sighed. How could he ask her about her husband's violence at home? He would never get a straight answer; then again, that told him everything he needed.

"If you can think of any other information about your husband that might be useful, you can call me at my office."

The line went dead.

Rex hung up the receiver and stared out at the crime scene. It made sense she wouldn't show concern about what happened to the woman that stole her voice; he would be suspicious if she did. But there was an undeniable mountain of evidence of Mr. Bailey's violent streak, even down to the busboy at The Neptune Club. He heard the fierce crashes upstairs. Billie must've witnessed his wrath first-hand. Yet the lounge singer still actively searched for him, even went as far as to defend his violent outburst.

A headache now pounding in his skull, Rex fastened his trench coat and stepped out in the growing evening cold.

Rex stepped from the chilly streets into the warmth of the Cordelia's relatively quiet foyer. Bernard Aldridge sat on the white sofa by the small fountain, chewing at his nails, eyes darting. Aldridge sweated bullets. He leaped from the couch, rigid like a frightened cat, when he noticed Rex. The detective slowed his gait across the foyer. Last thing he wanted to do was startle the man.

The fountain splattered in Rex's ear as he shook Bernard's sweaty hand.

"Mr. Aldridge," said Rex. "I thought we were going to meet in the apartment, like last time."

He shook his head. "We can't."

"And why not?" asked Rex.

"Because of what you said on the phone. You know, about the photo."

"The one with Mr. Bailey and Caroline? What does that have to—" Rex paused. "You were there. You were the one that took it."

The whites of Bernard's eyes came out as Rex pieced it together. It was hardly a damning admission of guilt. He was already friends with the woman, but the photo had him on edge like a confession note in his handwriting.

Rex cleared his throat. "So that whole thing about being mad Caroline took all the press for the musical was just a charade for your sister?"

"You can't tell Betty about this," said Rex. "If she knew that I was with them that weekend—"

Bernard trailed off, casting a bug-eyed glance over his shoulder like Ralph, the paranoid dope fiend in *Reefer Madness*. Yet the man seemed perfectly sober, intoxicated only with sheer terror.

"What would Betty do?" asked Rex. "Would she do something to you? Maybe even to Caroline?"

Bernard rubbed his fingers together then dropped back onto the white couch. He lowered his voice as he spoke to Rex. So quiet against the fountain, Rex had to sit and ask him to repeat. The detective was a little taken aback as he sat on the sofa, which was how he imagined sitting on a cloud would be. But when he swiveled over to Aldridge, the kid was anything but comfortable.

"I don't know," he whispered, as though he seemed to think Betty was over his shoulder. "I think my sister means well with her comments, but who knows what she's capable of."

"What makes you think that?" asked Rex.

"This is crazy, and I'm sure it means nothing," Bernard shot another glance over his shoulder. "But the night Caroline disappeared, Betty decided to intervene in her relationship with Mr. Bailey. Caroline refused, and Betty told her if she continued to see Mr. Bailey, she would wind up dead in some seedy lot somewhere. I feel silly even suggesting it, but after that, a severed finger turns up in the lot across the street from our apartment building. You couldn't blame a guy for being a little suspicious."

"But why not just tell the cops?" asked Rex. "Why bother telling me about it?"

"Because we don't know if she did it." Bernard ran a hand through his dark hair as he slid his forehead into his palms. "It's nothing more than a gut feeling at this point. Besides, that cop's already got it out for Betty."

Rex's heartbeat quickened at the mention of the cop. Benson had already been through all the papers bragging about the case; he also didn't waste time harassing Billie Bailey. Stood to reason that he would try and threaten a confession out of the nearest suspect.

"Let me guess," said Rex, "cocky kid, even younger than you? A nasty attitude?"

"That's the one," said Bernard. "He threatened us. Told us if we didn't confess to the murder, he would make sure Betty would spend her life behind bars when he actually caught her."

Just the kind of solid police work he expected from a rich kid like Benson. The outcome was more significant than justice. The world was black and white when looked at through a silver spoon.

"Look," said Rex. "I know you're trying to protect your sister, but I need to speak with Betty about this."

"I can't let you do that," said Bernard with an uncharacteristic sternness. "Betty is asleep upstairs."

"Already?" asked Rex. "Seems a little early. There were kids still playing outside."

Rex considered Bernard's story as the last rays of golden light crept behind the buildings outside the large glass doors outside the foyer. It seemed a little early to hit the sack. What could he be hiding? Even Rex's imagination felt it was a stretch that he bumped his sister off. Still, there was no way he could get up to the apartment without Bernard's approval, and that wasn't coming any time soon.

"So, can you tell me more about Mr. Bailey then? Anything you didn't feel comfortable saying around Betty."

"Not really," Bernard shrugged. "They were a pretty normal couple. They behaved like a pair of newlyweds, but I suppose all relationships start that way."

Rex cocked his brow. "And you never felt jealousy as an ex-lover?"

"Betty oversold that. We were just a couple of kids."

Rex went through the mental math in his head, and if they met Caroline after they got to LA, they wouldn't be deemed kids by any metric. Still, maybe there was some truth in what he said, and they remained good friends.

"How did Caroline feel about Mr. Bailey's wife?" asked Rex.

"How do you imagine she felt?" Bernard scoffed. "She made up all these vicious rumors about her. She gossiped that Billie was having an affair with Jimmy, which I don't believe. Billie doted on her husband, and he rarely showed her affection back."

Rex didn't share Bernard's optimism after his phone call to the lounge singer. Another man was with her. No doubt Rex had interrupted them in the throes of passion. It might even explain Billie's anger. Could it have been rage from the interruption, or perhaps her devotion stemmed from guilt? Maybe she accepted all those beatings as penance for her sins.

"And what about Mr. Anthony?" asked Rex. "He spoke to me about his passion for keeping bloodlines clean. You think he had anything to do with it?"

"Funny you should say that," said Bernard. "I've tried calling him a few times since you left here, and he hasn't answered. You don't suppose something has happened to him?"

Bernard's imagination seemed wilder than Rex's.

"Let's not get out of hand. I'll go and visit Mr. Anthony. Can you give me a home address? I need to ask him a few questions."

"Sure," said Bernard. "And thanks for being so understanding about Betty."

Rex smiled. He wasn't exactly sure how much choice he had in the matter, considering her brother locked her up in his golden tower away from the public. Bernard flashed a smile back as Rex stared into the white of his bugged-out eyes.

Rex hobbled down the steps of the Cordelia into the cold street. He tucked his hands into the pocket stood under the flickering lamp post in the dark, staring at the darkened lot. There was very little light, that was true, but it still seemed unlikely somebody could hack somebody's finger off without any of the neighbors noticing, even in the dead of night.

A sudden crunch reverberated against Rex's skull, and he dropped to the ground. He padded the still-warm pavement as the city streets spun. He made out a figure dressed all in black, a balaclava over his head through his hazy vision, getting into a busted Chevy.

Chapter 15

A hazy fog swirled inside Rex's skull like gasoline fumes as he tore down Crenshaw. The bright lights of gas stations and carwashes blurred past, a hyperactive merry-go-round spinning so fast it might fly off. A dizzy spell tossed his brain around like a swimmer trapped in a riptide. Cars floated over the paved streets, their red taillights shining in Rex's eyes, pulling his focus, but he honed in on the single maroon Buick in front of him. He could only stay one step ahead, and at the moment, that meant not plowing his Pontiac into somebody's living room.

Rex charged past the Buick, almost scraping its shiny new paintwork, not to mention his own. Drivers screamed. Honks blared. But the whole scene was muffled like it was underwater.

He would only focus on the car in front of him until he overtook it, then the next one. Eventually, he would finally catch up with the driver in the beat-up Chevy.

It was Carl Bailey. It had to be. Nobody else in LA would have the gall to drive around in that hunk of junk. He was the one that threatened Rex with that flyer, and now the thug made good on his promise.

The clues floated around his brain like somebody had stuffed his skull with helium. He shook his head in the hopes it would organize his jumbled thoughts.

The driver was long gone.

Rex slowed to thirty miles an hour. Rex didn't need horsepower. He needed brainpower, the very thing his concussion had taken from him. Carl Bailey was driving down Crenshaw onto Vine; only one place he could go.

"The Neptune Club," Rex shouted, veering off the road slightly, then making a sharp correction.

The jury was still out on Mrs. Bailey. Was he going there because he and his wife were in cahoots? Or was he coming back to punish her for reaching out to the detective? Rex didn't have the mental energy to weigh that up, but he needed to get inside the club regardless. The answer to solving the case was waiting there for him. Honestly, he was still hoping for the one that might provide a payout, but he needed to know either way.

Out the corner of Rex's eye, a black tabby darted across the street and froze. It just stared. Rex slammed the brakes, and the car fishtailed to a stop, mounting the curb with a clunk. He jerked forward, his chest pounding into the steering wheel. He groaned as he regained his breath. The tabby dashed back to the lawn it came from and licked its paw, wiping it over its head. Perhaps it was the concussion talking, but it was almost like the little son of a bitch did it to mess with him. Rex pounded his fist on the steering wheel and screamed. Most men would've just mowed down the little kitty. Even though Rex hated the little critters, he couldn't do it.

For the briefest second, he saw his drunk mother's white Persian on the hood of the car. Both his mother and the cat were long dead, and if Rex didn't watch himself, he'd probably get pulled over by the cops, and they'd lock him away in some looney bin. Then again, the brick might have done more damage than he realized. Maybe he *should* be headed for the booby hatch.

He shot the tabby a glare as it continued to groom itself on the lawn. Then Rex glanced over his shoulder and backed out onto the street. As he took off, theories restarted in his head. His minor run-in with the cat was inconsequential. He didn't have time to lick his proverbial wounds or patch up his literal head injury. The only thing that mattered was getting to the Neptune Club. The only thing he wanted was a Gin Rickey back at his office. The cool ice clinking in the jar, soda water sizzling against the lime slices, shooting the piney scent into the air. But he pushed the ice-cold drink out of his mind. He needed to save a woman's life or catch her out in a lie.

He screeched onto Sunset, speeding through the intersection and past his office. As The Neptune Club rolled into view, people lined up around the brown brick building, all gussied up in their finery. No sign of the Chevy. Rex puttered past, scanning the customers, but the crowd was decidedly white. Probably all gawkers after the news broke of Caroline Lake. They all wanted to see the wife of a killer like some freak show attraction.

Rex pulled up and reached for the door handle but stopped. He clicked open the glove compartment and rooted around until he found his new Colt 1911. Vow be damned, the detective had to protect himself. He was trying to be a better person. He wasn't suicidal.

He exited the car, stowing the gun in his belt loop, concealing it under his trench coat. Warm bulbs flashed in sequence around the marquee with Billie's name on it below the glowing red neon that proudly displayed the club's name. Wrinkled yellow posters of the woman stuck to the walls, her cool smile intoxicating the patrons as they gossiped amongst themselves.

Rex was less concerned with the glamour and more worried about finding a way into their home. There had to be side access to the rear of the lounge. At the end of the two-story building lay a narrow alley. Rex followed it to the end, where he met his greatest enemy: a knee height fence. He lifted his right knee with a wince as a million knives scraped against the bone. Still, he pushed through and planted his foot over the other side, then the left, which was worse. The detective climbed over and braced himself with the steel barricade with a white-knuckled grip for fear his legs may give out underneath him. He clutched the rough bricks and peered around the corner at the cramped concrete yard.

Over by the wire gate, the black Chevy's hood was visible, wrapped around an evergreen pear tree, smoke spewing from the crushed engine. As expected, he was too late, not that it helped the pit in his stomach. Rex hobbled to the olive-green pine door, which sat open as the screen banged in the chilly breeze. Rex drew the Colt with two hands as he stepped inside.

An eerie silence blanketed the laundry in the back, barely big enough to fit a basin and a musty mop. Beyond the laundry, the maroon wallpaper corridor continued down to a set of double doors with a painting or a rubber hose cartoon version of the sea god. But off to the right was a staircase that undoubtedly led to their living quarters.

A muffled thump traveled down the stairs. It could've been anything. A door slamming to a cat knocking a book to the floor, but who was he kidding? Fate was a cruel bitch. Of course Carl would've gone up the mountainous staircase.

He staggered up the staircase to a windowless olive-green corridor, practically pitch black except for a gold lamp on the hallstand. Rex, feeling his bones were nothing more than hot dust searing through his bloodstream, limped to the first door and slowly turned the handle. The door released and creaked open on a living room as light from the sign outside filtered through the blinds in blood-red horizontal stripes. Rex scanned his pistol across the tiny room, from the plush loveseat to the 7″ Viewtone in the corner. The space was empty.

He dry-swallowed as he left the room, then stopped in his tracks. The door beyond the hallstand had a crack of red light escaping out the bottom. Rex tip-toed over and pressed an ear to the pine door. Nothing but the hauntingly dulcet tones of Tommy Dorsey's *I'll Never Smile Again.*

Rex breathed deep, helped on, and twisted the door open, which slammed against the wall startling the detective. Gunshots echoed in his head as he swung the gun erratically to check all the hiding places. Maybe it was because of the red light that flooded through the open curtains, looking as though it soaked the entire room in blood, but it took Re a few moments to realize there was a body in the bed; blood-stained sheets hung over the head.

He lowered his gun and collapsed against the wall. It had all been for nothing. Carl came for his wife, and he got her. All because he was too old and feeble for the job. Perhaps if Rex had refused her, she might have taken on someone younger who could've saved her.

Then his pity turned to rage as he imaged the smiling monster in the photo. He had these women wrapped around his little finger. Bailey was willing to defend him until the final moment.

A crash came from the bathroom, and Rex aimed his pistol at the door. With his car out of commission and seemingly no options left, of course the little weasel would hide in the bathroom. He was big enough to push a couple of tiny women around, but when it came to a real fight, he was ready to hide like a puppy with its tail between its legs.

But the monster was still in the house, and concussion or not, Rex would bring him to justice. He wanted to fire two shots through the door, one for Caroline, one for Billie. But that was too good for him. Rex was confident his cellmate would do far worse and for much longer.

"Come out now," he called.

"Is that you, Mr. Horne?" called a smooth voice.

"Billie?" said Rex. "Open the door."

A gentle click. Mrs. Bailey stepped out in a shimmering green mermaid gown that fanned out at the edges. Her face grew pale as her stunning eyes sparkled at Rex. As she reached out for him, blood dribbled from the gash that sliced down her right forearm. She collapsed to the floor.

"I'll call an ambulance," said Rex.

He scanned the room and noticed a phone on the bedside table. He hobbled over, picked up the receiver, and punched in 0. There was a clunk.

"Operator, I need an ambulance," he screamed down the phone line.

"Just a moment, sir," said a chirpy voice from the other end. "Patching you through now."

Another click. Another voice.

"How can I help?" said the operator.

"No ambulance," Billie mumbled.

There had to be a reason she didn't want the ambulance to come. The cops would come, and surely Benson had thrown his weight around at the precinct to be the only person to deal with anything concerning The Neptune Club. No doubt it would cause negative attention towards the club, and if the detective was honest, he wasn't thrilled with the idea.

Rex slammed down the receiver. "Stay with me, Billie!"

"Sir, an ambulance will be with you shortly. Please stay calm and try to help us."

Rex returned to the singer and hollered as he crawled to the floor. He tore the bottom of the green dress off, wrapped it around the singer's arm, and tied it off. With too much pressure on his knees, Rex collapsed against the cool tiles, staring out the doorway at the blood-soaked bed. Amidst all confusion and concussions, he had forgotten about the body under the sheet. If it wasn't Billie, who was it?

"Mrs. Bailey?" called a voice from outside the bedroom.

"In here," Rex pressed against the woman's wound. "Help!"

The waiter Rex had interviewed charged into the room, brandishing a knife. The shaking blade glinted in the red light as his eyes widened.

"What is happening?" he asked.

"She was attacked," said Rex.

"No kidding," said the waiter. "But by who?"

"Santa Claus," Rex snapped. "Who do you think? Her husband! Now get me a first aid kit!"

The waiter disappeared for a couple of minutes. Billie Bailey's eyes rolled back into her skull as she drifted to sleep. Rex gave her a gentle slap on the cheek, and it seemed enough to pull her out of it.

"Keep talking to me," said Rex, fighting his own concussion. "Why don't you tell me about the gent under that sheet? Is it Carl?"

Billie shook her head.

"Jimmy Evans, is that it?"

Billie whimpered. "Will."

"Will what? Is that the man's name? Who is will Miss Bailey?"

But Billie didn't answer. Instead, she closed her eyes, and her head limped to one side. The room started to spin, and as hard as Rex fought, his eyelids grew heavy he felt the pull of sleep.

Chapter 16

A pleasant warmth radiated over Rex's midsection, traveling to his toes. He groaned as he stirred on a cushioned surface. It was so soft, the detective imagined himself in heaven, sitting amongst the clouds, then gave a hoarse snigger; men like him didn't end up in heaven.

Click. The brassy trumpets of Artie Shaw's *Stardust* played at a barely audible volume. Like some silver screen final act where the hero wakes up to discover it had all been a dream, Rex's eyes opened as the strings section swelled.

The white room was so glary Rex had to squint as his eyes adjusted. A dark shape rummaged around the foot of his bed.

"Billie?" asked Rex, his voice coming out feebler than he would like.

"Silly old fool," a husky British voice answered. "Honestly, can you take your mind off the job for one second?"

Virginia came into focus as she walked around the bed, primping the vase of fresh peonies, fiddling with the Philco wireless radio. As she turned to him, her raven-black hair cascaded over her shoulders in waves. Her dark hair was almost lost in the puffy-sleeved black number she wore. Naturally, it had gold buttons so the actress couldn't fade into the background, as though there was a chance of that happening. Her eyes were slathered with enough charcoal makeup to look like she had been in a bar fight. Rex chewed his lip to fight a smile. He didn't know why he would expect any less. He goes into the hospital with a mild concussion, and Virginia goes into mourning.

Virginia circled to the other side of the bed and took his hand, massaging it with her smooth fingers, her sharp nails scraping his rough hands so gently they almost tickled.

"There's my Rexy." She slowed her speech as though she thought him a dullard. Although, there was something comforting in knowing she would stay if he were. "Sweetie, you are at County Hospital. It seems that you hit your head."

"Gee, Virginia, I had a concussion, not a stroke." Rex chuckled.

Virginia stopped stroking his hand but tightened her grip. "I'm so glad to see you awake. The staff here have been incredibly unhelpful. All I did was tell the doctor that I would like to have you transferred to Queen of Angels to receive the best possible care, and suddenly, I am the villain. Is it a crime to want the best for the people I care about?"

Rex could imagine how Virginia's love manifested itself, screaming down the halls for a doctor, probably tossing herself on the floor for good measure.

Still, nice to be wanted.

His euphoria wore off as the last fog of sleep lifted, recalling the events at The Neptune Club the night before. Billie's face appeared in his mind, head tilted to one side, unresponsive.

"What about Billie?" asked Rex.

He shot upright, instantly regretting the decision. Virginia placed a hand on his shoulder and gently pushed him back against the soft pillow, not that Rex was going to fight her on it. He barely had any more strength than a kitten.

"Now, now," said Virginia. "You don't want to get yourself all riled up. Just calm down."

"But what happened to Billie?" Rex paused before he could as the question festered in his mouth. "Is she—"

"Has this become an obsession with the case or the singer?" teased Virginia. "Do I need to worry about you running off with some starlet?"

"Enough games," Rex barked.

"She's fine." Virginia tilted her head with a smile. "I was just talking to Benson. He said it was barely a scratch. They cleaned her up and gave her something to eat and drink. He even ran a full interview with her about her husband."

Cool relief washed over him like a wave, only for it to sweep his sleep and drag him under. He cleared his throat as he tried to breathe in without alerting Virginia. Did she say Benson had spoken to her? Did he come to her house? Was the vice cop there in the hospital? The last thing he needed was another scene that might get him kicked out of the hospital. And it wasn't like it was his first time with one of his little turns. He'd had them off and on since returning from Brittany. He just clenched his jaw and breathed deeply until it passed.

"Wait, Benson is here?"

Rex trembled until it felt like his bed was rocking, like his fighter plane did as it plunged towards the scarred ground.

"Darling, there's no need to get upset. The man is simply doing his job."

"Get him out of here," Rex grunted.

130

"He is just doing his job. You were there, at that horrible place where that poor appliance salesman was murdered."

Rex remembered the body under the sheet, splattered with blood.

"Will," said Rex. "She said his name was Will."

"Will Baker," said Virginia. "Baker's Electric. He owned three stores across locations Los Angeles."

Rex remembered the first time he set foot in The Neptune Club. Billie chatted to an appliance salesman. Rex only remembered him as a faceless man; there wasn't anything particularly memorable about him, but that must've been Carl's latest victim. Was it the first time they met or a preorganized excuse? Either way, it seemed odd the owner of the chain personally delivered a couple of hundred-dollar refrigerators.

"She was having an affair with him," said Rex.

"Little hussie," Virginia snapped. "Although it doesn't take a world-class detective to figure out that one. Good girls pay for their fridges with money, not their bedroom."

Rex ignored Virginia's barbs. "And more importantly, it gives Carl Bailey more than enough motive."

"Man wants to get revenge for someone sleeping with his woman," said Virginia with a shrug. "Tales as old as time."

"Well, Billie almost died last night because of that bastard. And the crazy thing is she defended him, right up until the moment he nearly killed her."

"It's like I said before. When someone makes you feel worthless, you'll do anything for them." Virginia placed a hand over his. "You're right about this whole thing. This poor girl was attacked, and I'm off making light of it like I'm Polly Whittingham or something."

They both shared a smile for a split second before the door opened, and Benson poked his head inside, offering a courtesy knock on the door.

"Mind if I come in?" he asked, then charged in before anybody could answer.

Benson strode into the hospital room like Humphrey Bogart or William Powell, though he shared none of the charms of his silver screen counterparts. The blonde kid strode over the bedside, jostling past Virginia, flashing his perfect straight smile. His glistening teeth looked as though they were slicked with oil. The corners of his mouth curved into sharp peaks like he was Vincent Price.

"How're you feeling, Major?"

Steadying his breathing, Rex offered a grunt and a shrug.

"I'll get right to it. I've got a couple of questions. Just got to tick all the boxes, you know how it is."

Benson turned to Virginia. He seemed to hope she would stew in the silence and excuse herself. Virginia stared back at him with a clever dumbfounded look on her face. Rex shot her a wink.

"Excuse me, little lady," Benson turned on his oily brand of charm. "Don't suppose you could give us a moment to catch up."

"It's alright, Mr. Benson." Virginia shot him a sly grin. "I can assure you if I focus extremely hard, my feeble female brain might be able to comprehend the question."

"Listen—" Benson dropped the pretense of politeness.

Rex pictured the reporter with the gun to his head, and rage spread through his body like wildfire, burning off any anxiety left in his throat.

"No, you listen, private," Rex barked. "She's not going anywhere, so if you don't want to pick your teeth up off the floor on your way out, you'll speak to the lady with some damned respect."

Virginia shot Rex a wink back as Benson tossed his nose in the air. Rex folded his arms in his bed. It felt damned good to put the little ferret back in his place.

"Very well," said Benson. "You might've just saved Mrs. Bailey's life. We believe you scared that monster away before he could finish the job on her too. But now, some other key players in this have gone missing. I have tried to contact Betty Aldridge, but her brother refuses to let me into their apartment. I'm still waiting on a warrant."

It seemed strange that Mr. Aldridge didn't crumble like a deck of cards the way he did with Rex. There was a strong force guiding his actions, but was it devotion to his sister, or was he trying to cover his own misdeeds.

"James A. Anthony and Jimmy Evans have also gone missing," he announced.

Rex sat up.

"That's terrible." Virginia held a hand to her chest. "What do you suppose happened to them?"

Benson ignored the actress' request and took a breath to continue.

"Private," Rex barked. "The lady asked you a question."

Virginia flashed him a smirk, then returned stern-faced to the detective as he reluctantly explained, like a child being forced to apologize.

"My guess is that these men were all guilty of something," said Benson. "But don't worry, ma'am, because I intend to bring them to justice."

Benson tipped his hat at the woman like some silver screen cop. Rex could see Virginia's respect for the man curdling in her eyes.

"You jackass," said Rex.

Virginia turned her back to him, no doubt to let out a chuckle at the vice cop's expense.

"Now listen here." Rex climbed out of bed, though not as gracefully as he imagined in his head. "And listen well because you might learn something. Those men might have done some things wrong, but they haven't run off in guilt. This is exactly the same as when Caroline Lake went missing in the first place. That monster Carl Bailey is out there. He has taken those men, and if you don't do your job right now, we're going to find their severed limbs scattered across LA."

"Major," Benson's voice dropped to a thin whisper, like a scolded child.

"I don't want to hear it," said Rex.

"But this is the opportunity we need," said Benson. "Clearly, there is so much you can offer us, and—"

"Good day, Mr. Benson." Rex returned to bed and folded his arms.

Benson stormed out of the hospital room. Virginia stood at the foot of his bed, arms folded. She shook her head, and Rex sighed. *Here we go.*

"Go ahead," Rex lifted a hand, offering her the floor.

"You're a stubborn old mule." Virginia shook her head.

"Let's not start this again," said Rex. "You heard what he did. I told you—"

"Of course, the man's a weasel," Virginia shrieked, then paused as she seemed to take stock, then dropped her voice to barely above a whisper. "You blind yourself with your hatred. You don't see what it does. Yes, Benson's a weasel, but at the end of the day, who're you hurting with this protest? He goes about his merry way as though nothing is wrong, and you sever yourself from a bank of information you could never get on your own."

Virginia's words resonated in Rex's skull. The more they echoed, the more truth rang in them.

"You've got a point," said Rex. "I've been looking at this whole thing wrong."

"Finally, you're starting to make some sense." Virginia threw her arms in the air with an exaggerated eye roll.

"Think about it. If Carl Bailey was hacking those people up to transport them or dump them around the city, whatever he's doing. That couldn't be a one-man job, right?"

Virginia threw her hands on her hips. "I guess not, but I really think you're missing the point of all this."

Rex dismissed her with a wave of his hand. "I know, but think about it. There was no way one man could do all that stuff. They had to be quick. Not to mention carting the bodies out of Brentwood like that, even in the middle of the night. That's no small feat. He had to have an accomplice."

Virginia leaned in, clearly still slightly miffed that he ignored her proposal to sign his soul to the cocky young devil, but it seemed like curiosity won the battle.

"One of your unreachable suspects is actually working with Carl Bailey. The real question is who?"

Rex humphed. "I have an idea."

Chapter 17

The gold doors clunked open on the cluttered penthouse apartment. Warm light filled the room, mingling with the harsh glow of Brentwood streetlamps outside. Perhaps it was the change of lighting, but it seemed as though the junk had multiplied. Were there this many photos and movie posters adorning the walls before? Was there a daybed still in the corner? Something about the room felt different. Then again, it could be the plates and magazines plonked onto the sofa. As he stepped inside, a musk hung over the room; not exactly filthy, but somehow unclean.

Bernard Aldridge greeted him at the door with what could almost be called a smile, the same as he did when they first met. Only this time, the grin was almost spooky. Something about the ghoulish man had Rex's flesh crawl. Grey bags hung under his eyes, and his skin had grown a waxy quality to it, like some nightmare creature from a Lon Chaney film.

"Mr. Horne," he said, a surprising level of warmth considering his sickly demeanor.

Rex flashed a half-hearted smile back, but he stayed perfectly still until the doors closed on another snooty bellhop with a high-pitched chime. Bernard seemed to stew in the silence, a smile on his face so tight it might crack his jaw.

"I'll be blunt, Mr. Aldridge," said Rex. "I'm here because I need to speak with your sister. You've been hiding her from me and even the police. Why?"

A million and one explanations raced through Rex's head like a fleet of Spitfires, but none of them painted a flattering picture of the composer. Bernard's body tensed as he clenched his fist, and the smile dropped from his face.

"Quite frankly, detective, what goes on with my sister is none of your damn business." he snapped. "I have been nothing but cooperative every time you and your little cop friend come sniffing around here. I answer your questions and put up with your thinly veiled accusations. And still, I'm the bad guy in all of this."

"I've never said you did anything," said Rex.

Bernard wasn't the sibling he was concerned with, although the little outburst may have pushed the composer a little higher up the list. Could he possibly have done away with his sister, tired of her racist rhetoric? Or was he the accomplice helping the man

"Of course you do. You all think I'm some creep—the full-grown man living with his sister. There must be something wrong with him. Is he dangerous? Maybe he's a confirmed bachelor." Bernard bent his wrist with a hand on his hip like a child performing I'm a Little Teapot. "Well, this may surprise you, but I would love to take a wife and have a whole gaggle of kids, but unfortunately, my sister went crazy."

Bernard Aldridge's body went limp as he collapsed beside the blue sofa and slid down to the floor. Tears glistened in his eyes as he stared up at the ceiling.

"I want to know the truth, that's all." Rex softened his voice.

"I don't mean to call Betty crazy," he wept. "I know she went through all that back in Cincinnati. It wasn't her fault."

"So, explain it to me then," said Rex as he moved over beside the couch. "Tell me what's happening."

"Betty isn't here," Bernard's voice rose to a squeak.

"Where is she?" asked Rex.

"I haven't got a clue."

Rex placed a hand on the man's shoulder. "You don't even have an idea?"

"I played nursemaid to my sister twenty-four hours a day since she was a teenage girl. After all this time, I was sick of being the responsible one. She took some Amytal and went down for the night. I thought I had the night to myself, so I went across the street to see *Bloomer Girl*. I hadn't seen it since the premiere, and it was nice to see Caroline again."

Bernard rose to his feet and made his way to the wooden cabinet by the far wall. He opened it and pulled out a bottle of whiskey, then plopped himself back on the floor. His previously perfectly groomed hair now swept over his forehead. He looked like a bum on a street corner with his rumpled suit and loosened tie.

"If I'm gonna get through this, I'm gonna need a little help."

Bernard tossed back the bottle and gasped for breath. He glanced up at Rex, who threw his hands up in a silent gesture to show no judgment from him. The detective would love to forget his troubles and toss back the bottle just as much as the composer, probably more. But he sat back and let the man speak.

"Because of Betty's..." Bernard paused as he seemed to search for the right words "*Condition*, I always have to be the strong one. But everyone forgets that Caroline and I were good friends. We might not be a couple anymore, but I never stopped loving her. So I went to see her in the only way I could. Of course, I wept like a little girl. And when I came back, she was gone."

Rex had to tread carefully for his next nugget of information. Bernard was like a clam about to snap shut at the slightest sign of danger. He patted the weeping man on the shoulder. Despite his stoic persona, Rex consoled many a young man after narrowly escaping death or watching their friends shot down in a fiery blaze.

"Weren't you worried when she disappeared?" said Rex.

"Not really. When I got back, the Amytal was sitting on her dresser. She obviously wanted to get away from me as much as I did her. It isn't the first time she's done something like this. She'll spend a few nights in The Hollywood Roosevelt, then come home with an apology."

While Rex bought the man's frustrated tears, he wasn't sure the composer understood the enormity of what was happening. Did he not realize the Caroline Lake situation wasn't an isolated incident? Did he know she was safe because he was Carl Bailey's accomplice, or worse yet, did he take care of her for good. Crazier things had happened. Perhaps his tears were guilt rather than grief.

"I think you need to find your sister, Mr. Aldridge," said Rex. "Carl Bailey is out there, killing people who wronged him, and it seems like Betty has plenty of reason to make his list."

Bernard Aldridge managed a snort as it seemed like the whiskey had sunk in its claws. He shook his head with a gnarled sneer.

"And that's another thing," he slurred slightly, then took another mouthful of the amber liquid. "Something about that whole story seemed wrong to me."

"How so?"

"It wasn't like I was the man's best friend, but I visited him and Caroline a few times up in San Francisco, and they were nothing but sweet to each other. Something about the picture doesn't add up."

"The man hit me over the head with a brick. We have a severed finger and a couple of celebrities missing. I've got the lump on my head to prove it."

"I'm not saying that didn't happen," said Bernard. "I just don't think it was Carl Bailey. The man I met was so sweet to Caroline, much better than I was when we dated."

"That might be so," said Rex, "but people's private lives rarely match up with their public ones. You should know that. You're in Hollywood, for Christ's sake."

"Maybe," said Bernard. "Or maybe the police and the press find it easier to pin the crime on the nearest colored man than finding the real culprit."

He had a point. Both Benson and Polly Whittingham didn't care about the truth, and if a colored killer made for a more palatable story for the public, why not destroy a man's life.

Still, the story didn't quite gel.

"But the busboy at The Neptune Club has heard Mr. Bailey smacking his wife around upstairs after closing time."

"Maybe you're right." Bernard took another sip, this time much smaller as the hooch seemed to hit him. "Just goes to show, you never truly know someone."

Rex's mind sparked with theories once more. Maybe Bernard was right. A person could spend most of your waking moments with someone and not know who they really are. Bernard said his sister had disappeared at least once before. Was it possible she left to kill Caroline Lake to prove she was right? A self-fulfilling prophecy. Rex cleared his throat and paused as he tried to find a way to ease Betty's whereabouts into the conversation.

"Bernard," Rex gripped his shoulder. "Let's say for a second that you are right, and somebody else is killing the cast and crew of *Bloomer Girl*. We have no idea what this person's motive might be. They might have no issue with Betty, but are you really willing to take that chance?"

Bernard rose from his spot on the floor and staggered back as the whiskey rushed to his head.

"You're right," he whimpered. "We've gotta find Betty."

"Exactly," said Rex. "And when you do, I need you to call my office and let me know you've found her. When she gets back here, I don't want you to let her out of your sights. If we can keep her here, I'll come back and talk to her, but right now, we have to keep her safe."

It was a half-truth. Perhaps Rex and Bernard did need to keep her safe, or maybe they needed to protect the cast of *Bloomer Girl* from *her*. Then an icy wave washed over him. Whether the killer was Carl Bailey or Betty Aldridge, both had the motive to go after the last person left on the call sheet. Either way, it pointed his investigation squarely at the same place.

Rex rose from his spot on the sofa's arm. Bernard staggered towards him.

"Where are you going?" he slurred. "You can't leave now. We gotta find Betty."

"Pour yourself a coffee, Mr. Aldridge. You'll be fine," said Rex. "But first, I need to use your phone."

"Why?"

"I've got to pay a visit to The Neptune Club."

Chapter 18

As Rex rolled down his window, the gathering gossips' murmurs rose over the white noise of distant traffic and horns screeching. Even though The Neptune Club was temporarily closed after the attack, it didn't stop a string of Busy Bettys from lining up outside the bar. Perhaps they weren't interested in the lounge act but were instead hoping to see the maniac come back for another stab at his wife; an off-putting anecdote to tell at dinner parties. Or maybe they considered themselves amateur Polly Whittinghams, vultures in training.

Now, the waiter's insistence on the phone that he came through the rear entrance made a whole lot more sense. Rex took the first right onto Gower and screeched his brakes as he almost missed the turn onto Harold Way. The narrow, evergreen-dotted side street was a borderline between the ugly two-story rears of every business on Sunset and the modest homes they overshadowed. Rex parked outside Tinseltown Apartments, a cracked stucco shoebox opposite the tree that lost the fight to Mr. Bailey's car. Rex climbed out of the Pontiac and walked past the slanted evergreen. Carl, or whoever was behind the wheel of that thing, was driving with some force; they wanted Mrs. Bailey dead.

Rex swung open the rusted gate and stepped into the concrete backyard, towards the wooden portico to the laundry.

As Rex reached for the door, a crash rang from the narrow alley running down the side of the lounge. The detective paused. His hyperactive imagination had been for a workout over the last couple of days, and perhaps his mind had invented it. Even if it hadn't, it was more than likely simply a cat on a trash can. Rex froze a moment, then the crash came again, a little fainter this time, but it was there.

Kitties didn't usually knock over trash cans twice.

Rex raced as fast as his burning legs would carry him to the knee-high fence. He caught a pair of legs sliding through a window fifteen feet away as he rounded the corner. Not enough to make an identification, but the neighbors hardly slipped through somebody's window in the dark to borrow a cup of sugar.

"Hey!" he screamed.

He hobbled back and pounded on the laundry door. He needed to at least make an attempt to be invited in. It was his third breaking and entering felony he committed, and he didn't exactly want to make a habit of it.

"Mrs. Bailey," Rex hollered. "You in there?"

Nothing.

It was another felony, and the third time might've made him a serial criminal, but he couldn't stand outside, waiting for an invitation when the poor girl was probably inside with a knife in her back.

Rex twisted the knob and swung the door open, regretting that in his desperation to return to The Neptune Club, he left his Colt in the glove compartment. Still, that precious couple of minutes it took to retrieve it might render the weapon obsolete.

As Rex stepped into the laundry, music trickled through the double doors at the end of the hall. A shaft of warm light projected onto the painting of Neptune, the fish-man with a maniacal grin better suited in some carnival house of horrors.

Rex couldn't make out the tune. The peppy tempo and trumpet squeaks seemed to thicken the tension in the air until it was stifling, like being trapped inside an oven, gasping for breath with nothing but an apple stuffed in your mouth.

Rex peered into the open door. A well-lit break room. Nothing particularly fancy; a small plastic table with an ill-fitted cloth draped over it and a fridge in the corner. But there was nothing of note inside; no inside murders, and no nooks where they could hide. The window remained open. The threadbare curtains hung in eerie stillness as the window overlooked the neighbor's cinder block wall.

Then it hit Rex, the music stopped. Rex left the room and headed for the lounge, but as he reached to push the swinging doors open, the music restarted, and Billie Bailey's voice filled the corridor again. Rex pushed the door open and stepped into the lounge.

Rex squinted as the harsh house lights bore down on him with the power of the desert sun. But even under the unforgiving lights, Billie Bailey glistened as she practiced a rendition of Duke Ellington's *Take the A-Train*. She swung her hips in a gold sequined knee-length dress, at odds with the white bandage wrapped around her left arm.

The singer belted and scatted all about taking the train back to Harlem. Rex stopped and watched the woman perform. A radiant smile spread across her lips as she showed off her vocal prowess to the empty. It was almost as though her uninhibited performance was like performing in front of the bathroom mirror; you could give it your all when nobody was watching. But Billie Bailey's voice had the whole of Tinseltown bumping gums. Her reservations seemed to come from the choice of song. Her typically white audience didn't want to hear her fast-paced jazz. While Rex had listened to some of the genres and even enjoyed a few songs, he still knew several people who thought it *colored* music; and jazz musicians nothing but a bunch of bums who sat around all day smoking reefer. But Billie seemed so at home performing the music her audiences derided.

"Mrs. Bailey," said Rex, but the woman continued. Rex almost felt bad for breaking it up. "Mrs. Bailey!"

Billie spun around to face the detective but lacked the range of motion in her form-hugging dress and tumbled onto her backside. She screamed as she dropped to the floor with a thump. Rex climbed onto the small stage and offered her a hand.

"I'm so sorry, Mrs. Bailey. I didn't mean to frighten you."

Her face seemed to relax as she noticed it was the detective. She placed a hand to her chest and let out a sigh.

"It's alright, honestly," she panted, trying to manage a smile. "I just thought I would hear you if you knocked on the door."

"I wasn't the only one you didn't hear," said Rex.

Rex killed the phonograph, and silence expanded in the room like shaving foam. Suddenly every bump and creak was like a firebomb.

"You don't suppose it's Carl?" she asked with a sick note of yearning. "I know what you must be thinking, but I worry about him."

Rex shook his head, but it was the only thing to stop him from shaking the crazy dame herself. After everything he did, how could she still hold a torch for such a bum?

The door slammed open from the opposite side of the hall. Rex flinched as Billie squealed again, gripping his fist with her trembling hand. The waiter charged in, armed with a Louisville slugger and a mad glint in his dark eyes.

"What's going on?" he shouted, glancing around the room as though for some intruder's benefit. "I heard screaming."

"It's alright." Billie raised her hands in the air. "We're okay, but Mr. Horne did say he saw someone. So maybe you should do a sweep of the house just to make sure."

The waiter clutched the baseball bat with both hands and rested it on his shoulder as he kicked the double doors open and walked into the semi shadowed corridor.

Rex ushered the singer to the nearest seat, and she sat upright, no longer the uninhibited woman performing on the stage only moments ago.

"I know what you're thinking," she said.

"What's that?" asked Rex, grunting as he lowered himself into his seat.

"You think I'm one of those pathetic bimbos waiting around for their husbands even though they treat them like dirt."

That sounded about right from Rex's understanding, but putting his foot in it wouldn't help anybody, so he kept his trap shut.

"But I didn't deserve him." She looked away, tears glistening in her eyes.

"You mean because of the affair?" asked Rex.

Billie stared at him, opening her mouth several times, but it seemed as though the words didn't quite form.

"I know he isn't faultless," she said, "Lord knows all of Hollywood knows that now. But—"

A perfect tear rolled down her cheek as she turned to the stage. She smiled, but it wilted as she sniffed back another sob.

"He proposed to me right there. We had been together since 37, but he never asked me to marry him. Well, I worried that maybe it was because he didn't like me. Turns out the damn fool was trying to save up his pennies to get me the ring he thought I deserved."

Billie flashed the gold band on her finger, with a moderately priced diamond in the center. The gem sparkled under the bright lights. Billie smiled as she stared into its hypnotic glow.

"But turns out the old saying was right," she sighed. "Go with your gut. Carl didn't love me, not the way he loved that witch Caroline Lake, as it turns out."

"So, you don't think that he had anything to do with what happened to Caroline?" asked Rex. "Even after he attacked you and sliced up your arm?"

Billie shook her head and turned her back to him. "You wouldn't believe me. You all think Carl is the bad guy in this."

"If Carl didn't attack you, then who did?"

"I didn't see," said Billie. "The room was dark when that maniac came in with the knife. It could've been anybody. It all happened so fast."

"But did anything happen that didn't suggest it wasn't your husband?"

"I did receive a phone call today," Billie chewed on her fingernails, her back still to the detective. "The voice was hard to make out like the person was whispering down the other end, but I heard when they said I was going to die tonight."

"And you didn't think to call the police?" asked Rex.

"Where I'm from, you call the police, and odds are they'll be the ones to shoot you." Billie scoffed. "Besides, I'm a singer in a lounge act. It's hardly the first time I've received a strange phone call."

"Was it a woman's voice?" asked Rex.

Billie spun around, makeup dribbling down her tear-streaked face. She stared at him, terror glistening in her dark eyes.

"How could you know that?" she asked. "Who is it?"

"Betty Aldridge," explained Rex. "She was a composer on - *Bloomer Girl*, and let's say she has *a grudge* on your husband. And now, it seems she's focused on you too."

Billie's face contorted as she seemed wounded by the accusation by proxy. Tears sparkled in her eyes as she looked dumbfounded.

"What could I possibly have done to this woman?"

"She is angry at the world and needs someone to blame." Rex shrugged. "I don't know what else to tell you."

The double doors by the stage swung open, and the busboy stormed in with the slugger still over his shoulder. He shook his head.

"I've checked everywhere. There's no sign of anyone. It seems that Mr. Horne scared him away."

"Or her," said Billie, casting the detective a glance.

The busboy returned to the kitchen as Rex rose onto his aching knees. Billie rose to meet him, gripping his sleeve with her right arm. She stared at him as though he held a gun to his head.

"You can't seriously be thinking of leaving me here."

"I have to find out where Betty Aldridge is," said Rex.

"You tell me some crazy white woman has climbed through my window and tried to kill me. *Twice!* And I'm supposed to sit here alone in this house."

Billie rose to her feet and paced the room, chewing on her fingernails as she seemed to frantically search for a plan to protect herself from the madwoman. Rex couldn't dump the bombshell on her and walk away.

He sighed. "I suppose I could check in on Mrs. Aldridge tomorrow. Maybe she'll come home, and it might turn out to be nothing. But would you mind if I use your phone? I really should call Virginia and let her know."

A weight seemed to lift from Billie's chest. "I don't think we can afford a long-distance call at the moment."

"No, Virginia is my—" Rex stopped himself. "Doesn't matter. It's a local call."

Billie led the detective to the phone at the front desk. The people still piled up at the front through the glass doors. If only they knew the gossip he did, they might have a conniption.

"Hello?" Virginia said down the other end.

Rex explained the situation, and though she seemed a little disappointed, she understood.

"I guess my fresh-made spaghetti bolognese can keep until tomorrow."

"I'm so sorry," said Rex. "I know work has been a lot at the moment."

"Just promise me one thing," said Virginia. "Catch that son of a bitch and get justice for poor Caroline."

"I'll try might best. I'll see you later."

Just as Rex was about to hang up the phone, Virginia's overmodulated voice came down the other end.

"Rex," she called.

"Yeah."

"It seems like all the crazies are converging on The Neptune Club at the moment, and I know you are there to protect Mrs. Bailey, but I please to take care of yourself, darling."

"I will, I promise."

Silence hissed from the other end.

"I love you," Virginia's voice crackled.

Was it genuine affection or fear that might be the last time they spoke that spurred on her words? Rex didn't want to dig deep enough to find the answer to that.

Rex smiled. "I love you too."

Chapter 19

Rex sat on the love seat in the upstairs living room as the city hissed like a sedated snake outside the window. He tapped his knee in anticipation, preparing for the moment when the attacker tried again, jostling the Colt in his hand. He may have been foolish enough to leave the pistol in the glove compartment once, but he wasn't about to spend a night in the deathtrap without it.

As the hours passed and the city was on the brink of sleep, his eyelids grew heavy. The rose-pink walls and green cabinets blurred in and out of focus. He tried turning on the Viewtone, but its blue glow only lulled him further to sleep. Rex rose from the comfortable sofa and paced the small living space. He then watched over the practically empty Sunset Boulevard.

Rex changed his mind. He wanted the killer to come by for Round Two. He could finally put the case to bed and maybe even go for forty winks himself.

Something about the Betty Aldridge theory didn't seem to gel; mental problems aside, it seemed a little farfetched to believe that she would go to such lengths to attack the wife of the man with whom her best friend ran away. The link was so tenuous Rex could barely piece it together with his sleep-deprived brain. The evidence against Carl Bailey was mounting; the violence he inflicted on his wife in the same space he now stood, the fierce outbursts on the set.

Now Rex was inside the prime suspect's home. His wife was asleep in the next room. He had the entire run of the house, and while a weight sunk in his gut, he would sell his soul to the devil to end the case and get some sleep. Besides, he got nowhere with Billie Bailey.

Rex thought back to the hall. Their living quarters weren't exactly huge. They had the small living space, the bedroom where Carl murdered Mr. Baker, but there was a third door. If there was any chance of finding clues to get inside Carl Bailey's head, they had to be in that room.

Rex peeked outside the door into the darkened hallway. Warm light came from the crack under Billie's bedroom door. The woman didn't want to sleep in the dark, not that he could blame her after the attack. After everything she had been through, Rex was sure the woman would be a light sleeper. He removed his wingtips and crept down the corridor in his socks, still conscious of every scrape that sounded like paper tearing in the silence.

Rex stepped onto a loose floorboard, and though he could feel it under his feet, he couldn't do anything but lean into it. The alternative was to tumble back and crash to the floor. The loose board creaked like a series of loud cracks, and Rex froze, staring at the door, trying to conjure a decent excuse. Perhaps he was just about to check on her, or maybe he heard a suspicious noise and came out to investigate.

Although the detective didn't need an excuse, the door remained still, the room silent. Rex returned to the door opposite and opened it, expecting the same loud creak, but it slid open with ease, and Rex stepped inside. The pink room was almost completely pitch black except for the shard of light from the singer's bedroom door.

Junk filled the room, which wouldn't seem out of the ordinary, although Rex suspected that most people didn't fill their spare rooms with pictures of themselves; posters, signed photos, and 8X10 headshots, all splashed with Billie Bailey's face against a yellow background. It probably wouldn't be unheard of to find this kind of stuff in some Hollywood homes, but Mrs. Bailey had said she didn't want any more of the spotlight. Billie was just happy singing her songs, a sight Rex had the rare fortune to behold earlier. From the dust the pictures collected, perhaps that was a dream she put to bed long ago.

Rex rooted around the room and found more of the same, but just as he was about to leave, he caught sight of a white steel box by the door, skirmishes of rust tracking over the top. Rex unclipped the metal chest and looked inside—a couple of dressings and a waxed pouch of BC headache powder. Tucked into the corner was a wadded bandage. Brown stains glued the fabric together—dried blood. He still didn't want to jump to conclusions. If he didn't stop himself, the mailman would end up on his list of suspects. What if it was a change of dressing? There was a lot of blood. When rex pulled the bandage out, it didn't move. The crusty old thing had been sitting there for a while. Billie had tucked this away to patch herself up after Carl's beatings. She couldn't go to the police, possibly out of worry for her safety or perhaps for fear of what they might do to her husband.

Another solution trickled into Rex's sleep-muddled mind, one that took into account the bandages and the publicity stills in the abandoned room.

Perhaps Billie told the truth about her lack of desire for fame. Maybe it was Carl that saw her as a commodity, like livestock. He had already been making a comfortable living off her lounge act for the longest time. Perhaps she protested, and he convinced her to do the movie with his fists. Then he tired of his wife and moved onto Caroline Lake, but she wasn't as malleable as Billie, so it didn't take as long for him to become violent with her. Perhaps she threatened to call the police, and suddenly the lovebirds were now locked in battle. But from all accounts, Carl Bailey was not a man to live alone. He needed a woman, a surrogate mother, to look after him and soothe his violent tantrums.

He returned to Billie, but he found her in bed with Mr. Baker. One would think that would be enough to push Carl away, but a man like him couldn't live alone. In desperation, he *would* return to Billie, maybe not tonight or the next, but he needed somebody to nurse him. Perhaps he would even return with some flowers and an apology. Rex shook his head. All the pieces fit, but the scariest part to Rex was the fact that likely, Billie would take him back, and the cycle would start again.

The only puzzle piece that didn't add up to him was Betty Aldridge's phone call. She threatened Billie, unable to disguise her voice as a woman. But the murders took place across the street from her home, not to mention she showed animosity for both Caroline and Carl. And while it might seem like a long shot, the woman had motive to kill the colored man. The attacks on Billie could be an attempt to cover her tracks. If she staged a home invasion, people would be sure to think Carl Bailey was alive and well, not hacked up in a box somewhere.

A headache thumped in Rex's skull as he poked another flaw in his theory. A tiny woman like Betty Aldridge wouldn't be able to lug two bodies around Brentwood, let alone without getting noticed. Perhaps she had an accomplice.

James A. Anthony.

Rex shook the thoughts from his head. He was about two minutes from suspecting himself as the killer. He desperately needed sleep.

Just as Rex left the room, a thump came from the ground floor. Rex grabbed his Colt and made his way down the stairs. He heard a smash, like a shattered window, when he reached the bottom. Rex crept through the double doors and hobbled across the darkened lounge. Now, the usually glittering space sat still, empty chairs and tables, giving the rectangular hall a haunted house vibe. Rex continued into the kitchen, which was lit only by a sliver of streetlight, enough to highlight the silhouette by the bench. Rex aimed his gun.

"Don't move!" he shouted. "Get on the ground."

A woman screamed, and the silhouette dropped to the floor.

"You idiot," Billie's unmistakable voice rang from the darkness. "For a moment, I thought you were that crazy woman, coming to finish the job."

Rex wasn't sure how he felt having his voice compared to a tiny woman's like Betty's, but he pushed that to the back of his mind.

"What are you doing wandering around in the dark?" Rex flicked on the light.

Billie winced, her freckled face free of makeup. "Because I'm not exactly show-ready, but thanks for bringing that up. In all the chaos, I didn't eat anything last night, so I thought I would stop by for a cookie, and you can see how well that went."

A plaster fish lay smashed on the floor, bulbous eyes and a thick-lipped grin, like something out of a *Toby the Pup* cartoon.

"I think it's safe to say nobody's getting any sleep in this house tonight." Billie pulled out a plate of cookies and held them out to Rex. "How about I make us a cup of Joe, and we have a little chat."

Rex smiled. "That would be lovely."

Rex didn't realize how much he needed a hot coffee until Billie sat the steaming mug before him. White steam curled above the cup into the lounge. The detective and the singer sat at the table opposite the stage, sipping their drinks in silence. What was left to talk about with the singer? Rex was confident she had more information on her husband, but it wasn't like she would divulge anything.

"Thank you," Rex muttered. "For the coffee, I mean."

"I can't tell you how many times they've kept me up through late-night shows or after a big night when Carl—"

She stopped herself and picked at her red nails as though it was the most pressing task in her life. It was hard to believe the woman was the same person who belted out on the stage only a few feet from where they sat. But that was the power Carl had over her.

While he far from approved of her affair with the married appliance salesman, he could empathize just wanting to find a distraction from a dead-end life. He couldn't count the amount of Gin Rickey's he'd thrown back for the same reason.

"If I'm frank with you," said Rex, "will you do the same for me?"

"Of course." Billie managed a teary smile.

"I did a little digging around tonight, and I saw the medical chest in the spare room, the one with the bloody bandage in it."

"Oh, that," she giggled. "That was nothing."

"No, it wasn't," said Rex. "He hurt you, hasn't he? Billie, I need all the facts if I'm ever going to solve this case and bring him to justice."

"I'd rather not talk about that," Billie turned away.

"You seem to hold this torch for the man, as though you deserve it."

"I do," said the singer, then clapped a hand over her mouth.

"You mean because of the man in your bed?" Rex paused as he weighed up whether to say the man's name. "William Baker."

"You must think I'm a common slut," she wept.

"No," said Rex. If he was honest, all he was hoping was to put the case to rest. "I'm not here to judge."

"You should," she sobbed. "I *have* behaved like a slut. And if I am being honest, I wasn't even interested in the man. I only have eyes for Carl, but I made that stupid mistake, and made him feel like less of a man."

The woman picked at her fingernails, and the constant clicking got on Rex's last nerve. He reached over to hold the woman's hand but knocked over his mud, and it spilled over the tablecloth, dribbling onto the floor. Billie rose to her feet, flicking a few drops from her hand.

"I'm so sorry," said Rex.

"It's alright," Billie moved to pick up the mug, but Rex stopped her.

"No," he said. "I made this mess. I'll clean it up."

As he crouched to pick up the mug from the floor, Billie's creamy arm skin almost glowed under her flowing nightgown. Flawless.

She wasn't wearing the bandage.

No scars.

No stitches.

It was her.

Chapter 20

Rex loosened his white-knuckled grip on the chipped mug. He dropped to his knees with a guttural grunt as white-hot pain vibrated against his joints. Didn't hurt that Billie was there to witness the pathetic display. His crumbling body might've just saved his life. Random thoughts and vague schemes crashed into one another. It was the wild west in his brain as escape plans, and silver screen endings flashed through his mind, but he couldn't hold onto one long enough before the next fantasy ending knocked it out of the way. There had to be a solution. He had got himself out of stickier situations, surely.

Maybe not.

"Everything alright down there?" Billie giggled, a voice smooth as butter.

"I've ruined your mug," Rex groaned. "I'm sorry. You bring me into your home, and all I do is destroy your things."

Rex contemplated a sob but decided against it. He was trying to act normal, not like Virginia. His heart almost leaped out of his chest. She knew his whereabouts, a fact Billie was all too aware of. Not to mention that Virginia would be down to The Neptune Club the second she sensed something was wrong. If the singer was truly unhinged, she could see Virginia as a threat.

Billie placed a soft hand on the detective's shoulder, and his blood turned to ice water. He smiled at the woman as he rose to his feet, leaning against the table.

"Sorry," he groaned. "Being an old coot isn't fun."

Rex flopped in his chair, gripping his knee with a wince. Considering the million hot needles poking into his joints, it didn't require much acting. Billie's face sagged in a frown as she reached out a hand for him. She seemed genuinely concerned, a trait he didn't expect in someone who had committed triple homicide. Was it a performance, or could there be a rational understanding? Seemed unlikely. There weren't many reasons you could murder three people and still come out the good guy.

"I have to ask. Why me?" Rex lowered his head, rubbing his burning legs. "There's a lot of private dicks in this city, plenty of them better than me. Younger too, with working knees."

Billie smiled at him and took a sip from her coffee. "Do you sing, Mr. Horne?"

"My mother always told me I sounded like a drowning cat," Rex sniggered. "Put a crimp in my plans of being the next Jimmie Rodgers."

"People think that if you hit the right notes, then you're a singer."

"Isn't that right?"

"It's part of it, sure, but you need the soul, the feeling. You sing only at the perfect pitch; everything's dull. But you also can't simply say the words with emotion, or you end up like *a drowning cat.*"

Rex settled back into his chair as he found himself enjoying the conversation. How could such a charming young lady be responsible for killing three people? But as hard as Rex backflipped in his mind, he couldn't conceive of any other reason why the woman might fake her injury. It confirmed she was at the very least responsible for Will Baker's death.

"So, how does one get a great singing voice?" asked Rex.

The woman settled back into her chair. Was she relaxed because she didn't suspect something, or was she confident she had him trapped in her web?

"Singing requires skill and finesse. You have to blend the technical and the emotional at once to deliver truly outstanding performances." Billie tilted her head to one side. "That's why I chose you. I followed the Cinderella case, same as everyone else in this city, and you were so different from the others. You weren't just the gun-wielding gumshoe from the movies, but you weren't some weeping nelly like Jimmy Evans, either. You took the best of both those qualities and combined them into something special."

Rex managed a smile. Despite everything, he couldn't help but be flattered by the lounge singer's words because they seemed so heartfelt.

"You sure I wasn't just lucky," Rex chuckled, shrinking into his shoulders.

"Compassion and protectiveness," said Billie. "That is how *you* sing, Mr. Horne."

Rex tried to find the contradiction in her coffee black eyes, some proof that it was all a long con, but there was nothing. As far as he could tell, she believed in him.

"Look," Rex stood up. "It's been very kind of you to stay up and chat with this old crank, but you need to get some rest. Why don't I take these and clean up?"

Rex grabbed the empty mugs and turned for the kitchen. He needed Billie to go back to bed so he could root around for more evidence.

"Nonsense," said Billie. "You are a guest in my home. I can't have you cleaning dishes for me *and* saving my life. Besides, do you think I could go to sleep after a cup of Joe that strong?"

Before he knew what was happening, Billie trotted side by side with the detective. She hooked her arm in his, and they both stepped into the kitchen. Rex scouted the white room. There were two doors. The one on the right seemed to lead into another alley on the opposite side of the building. The one on the left, beside the refrigerator, was secured with a chunky padlock. Whatever answers he needed were locked in that room.

Billie released her grip from the detective as he hobbled to the blue bench and placed the mug in the sink. But then he looked up. Billie's reflection stood behind him, holding a pistol at her hip as they did in the movies. Rex hoped that meant she didn't have experience with it. Much easier to escape an amateur marksman.

He spun around. The singer aimed a Colt 1911 square at his chest.

His Colt.

Chilly sweat dribbled down his forehead as the room spun. The answer was just out of reach; there were still pieces missing. Every fiber in his body told him to run for the kitchen door, but he couldn't. He was so close to figuring it out. It wasn't about the money anymore. Rex's chances of getting paid had long flown out the window, but he needed to know why. Find out what made the woman tick.

"I wouldn't bother heading for the door," said Billie, erratic tension in her voice. "The previous owner was paranoid, thought the commies were going to come in the middle of the night and kill him, so he bricked it up. You can't leave."

"You don't have to do this," said Rex, holding his hands in the air.

"You think I want to?" said Billie. "I'm not some screwy loon who gets her kicks from killing people."

"So why did you do it then?" asked Rex.

"That's the thing about men, isn't it?" Billie shook her head. "You all think the world revolves around you. Do you think this is *Eyes in the Night* or *The Maltese Falcon*? This is real life. This isn't the moment where I tell you my dastardly plan to take over the world so that you can undo everything. The real world is messy, difficult, and full of impossible choices. I made mine, and it's too late to turn back now."

Billie sidestepped across the kitchen, refusing to remove her aim from the detective. Clever move since Rex would've taken any opportunity to take the gun from her. She pulled a key from her pocket and tossed it to the floor.

"Pick it up," she shouted. "Slowly. No funny business."

Rex picked up the key, eyes closed, breathing through the pain.

"Now open it," she ordered.

Rex shuffled over and jiggled the key into the lock, but it stuck. He tried to pull it out, but it wouldn't budge. Heart in his throat, the detective bashed the key against the door.

"You have to be gentle with it," she said. "Go easy."

Rex softened his grip on the key and twisted, and the lock clicked open.

"Billie, please," said Rex. "I know you don't want to do this. There's gotta be a way we can work this out."

"Don't do that," her face pinched as tears dribbled down her cheeks. "Don't make this harder than it already has to be. I'm sorry, but I can't help you."

Rex gently pulled the key from the lock.

"Open the door," Billie ordered.

"You don't--"

"Open it!" the woman shrieked.

Rex opened the door. A long staircase descended into inky blackness.

Billie ran her free hand through her jet-black hair. "You have to go downstairs while I try to figure this out."

As she paced, Billie tapped the side of the pistol against her forehead as though that might tease out the idea. Rex saw a chance, and he lunged at her. But like a rattlesnake, the singer shipped into action and fired. A flash of white light. A hot sting in his shoulder. Rex thumped into the doorframe, then tumbled down the stairs into the darkness. He landed on the hard concrete with a slap. From the top of the stairs, the singer's silhouette visibly trembled.

"Billie, don't!" Rex shouted, but the singer closed the door with a thump that rang through the darkness.

Chapter 21

The black void sat still except for a mechanical hum from the shadows. Rex groaned in the dark, his cheek pressed against cold concrete, while the bullet wound in his shoulder burned. He was almost glad he couldn't see.

Rex pictured Virginia as they delivered the news to her. Her melodramatic response didn't make him smile. Instead, the image stabbed into his chest like an icepick. A tingle went through his body as the room spun like he was stuck to the concrete block, aimlessly turning through space.

He mustered the energy to roll onto his back in the hopes it might slow the bleeding.

"You alright?" said a familiar voice.

"Mr. Horne?" called another.

At first, Rex figured he must've become delirious from the blood loss, but a flashlight beam cut through the darkness, illuminating James A. Anthony's freckled face. He wore a crumpled brown suit, and his balding ginger hair puffed out in frizzy waves, though the basement didn't have anything to do with that one. Bags hung under his eyes. The director had been down in the cellar for at least a couple of days.

Jimmy Evans scuttled over to the light, his skin pale, his usually impeccable dark hair flopped in messy strands over his forehead.

"Sorry about the cloak and dagger routine," said Anthony. "We weren't trying to give you the willies or anything. We have to save the batteries on this thing. There aren't any windows in this place, so some light would be nice."

Rex sat beside Anthony and Evans at the pseudo campfire.

"Did you spill the coffee as a distraction to get away?" asked Anthony. "Was that when you figured it out?"

Rex furrowed his brow.

The director shot him a smile. "You'll forgive an old man his indulgences. Listening in on conversations like a couple of peeping Toms is the only thing keeping us sane."

"But how—"

"The ducts," said Jimmy Evans. "We hear everything that goes on in this house of horrors. Including that jezebel and her defiling of the sanctity of marriage."

James A. Anthony's smile dropped, his flabby cheeks sinking like a sad clown. "We had to hear her kill the poor man too."

"Why did she do it?" asked Rex, gripping the bullet wound in his shoulder.

"We still don't know," said Evans. "I guess we never will. Not until we're reunited with our Lord."

"So, how did you both end up here?" asked Rex.

"She told me Carl was in a bad way," said Anthony. "She said he came in with a headwound and dropped to the floor."

"And that didn't sound odd to you?" asked Rex.

"I don't think I would've recognized Carl without a bandage on him. He always seemed to get into scuffles in some dive bar. He'd never tell me where, but he'd always stagger home, and Billie would patch him up."

"It sounds like there is a pattern."

"But you didn't know Carl the way I did," said Anthony. "He was the sweetest, most thoughtful guy I knew, even if he did indulge in predilections with Caroline that make me physically sick."

Just when Rex was starting to enjoy the man's company, Anthony's spiteful side crept out. Rex stared up at the ducts. The violence the waiter heard; Rex had broken the first rule of being a detective.

He assumed.

"Carl never laid a hand on her, did he?" said Rex, guilt sinking into the pit of his chest.

James A. Anthony shook his head.

"But Billie was the one with a bit of a temper."

"That's going a bit far," said Anthony. "No way a little lady like that could give him that kind of pummelling."

The man's pale face stared at him through the darkness, a red welt rising near his left temple.

"Who gave you that mark on your head?" asked Rex.

"Fair point," Anthony shrugged. "But I know Billie. She wouldn't just beat the crap out of him for the hell of it."

"She wanted him to have a reputation for being a brute," Rex explained. "That's why she must have taunted him with her affair, made him think it was Jimmy. The quietest ones always nap the loudest, and she made sure it was in a very public place."

Anthony shook his head. "But why would Carl go along with it?"

"How many men do you know are going to fess up that their wives beat them up?"

James A. Anthony's face sunk. He probably went through all the times he could've helped his friend if only he picked up on the signs.

"But she was so nice to me. We talked about my music and—"

The crooner's words echoed as Rex remembered Billie's scornful glare in the kitchen.

"You think the world revolves around you," Rex muttered the words.

"I beg your pardon," Evans snorted.

"That's what she told me," said Rex.

"He's telling you she played you like a fiddle, genius," said Anthony.

Still, Rex couldn't focus on the argument, not when all the pieces of the case were clicking together before his eyes.

"What about you, Jimmy?" asked Rex.

Jimmy Evans cleared his throat, clearly still wounded. "She came to me and asked me to share the story about Carl's attack with The Hollywood Scoop, just like she convinced me to tell the truth about Caroline. But after seeing the damage it caused the first time, I wouldn't do it. But then I started asking questions. There was so much that didn't make sense. Why was she obsessed with seeing justice against Carl? Couldn't she let it go? It happened to me, and I had forgiven the man."

Jimmy Evan's body tensed, folding his arms against his chest as he seemed to relive the moments in silence. He opened his mouth to speak but seemed to stop himself. Perhaps he couldn't find the words, or maybe he didn't want to admit he was stupid enough to let a woman snare him in her basement.

"It was the day I first met you. After you left, she asked me if I could help move the fridge in the basement, but she locked me in when I got down here. Told me I knew too much, asking too many questions."

"That's why she's doing all of this," said Rex. "She's scared of getting caught. Now she's trapped in a vicious cycle to cover her tracks."

"Maybe," Jimmy shook his head as he stared over his shoulder. "But all I keep thinking is about how stupid I was. She already moved the fridge."

Rex's heart thumped so loud it almost detracted from the most significant puzzle piece.

"The fridges," said Rex, slowly, as the last details of the murder percolated in his brain. "The fridges are key to the whole thing."

"How?" James A. Anthony scoffed.

"Because that's where Carl and Caroline are?"

Silence hung over the room as the men each turned to the two powder-blue GE refrigerators. The silver chains wrapped around them glistened in the flashlight beam. The men stared in silence. The three of them lowered their heads out of respect.

"How could you know that?" Anthony's voice cracked.

"The night she died, Caroline Lake went to see Betty Aldridge in Brentwood. Billie must've confronted the two of them, but she couldn't kill them right then and there, so my guess is she drugged them. Probably chloroform."

"But how could she attack two people like that. It would've caused a scene."

"She didn't do it by herself," said Rex. "She had help from a little lap dog who would do anything for her. Will Baker."

"There's a Baker's Electric in Brentwood," said Jimmy Evans, "across the street from the Cordelia, next to that empty lot where they found the finger and that jewelry."

"Left there deliberately to frame Betty Aldridge."

Jimmy Evans shook his head. "This is almost unbelievable."

"That's not the worst part. Billie and Baker had to dispose of the bodies, and if it were just Carl, they could dump his body on the racist's doorstep and leave. Carl would be lucky if his case made it to the desk of a decent LAPD cop, and even if it did, the evidence against Betty was pretty damning. But they had killed one of the most talked-about actresses in Hollywood. They needed to hide the bodies until the heat was off them. Somewhere cool."

"So they shipped them here in these two fridges?" asked James A. Anthony, his voice fragile as though on the brink of tears.

"Seems like Billie wouldn't even let them be together in death."

A chill tingled over Rex's skin as he tried not to think too hard about what it took to get the cheating couple to the basement. Each step seemed more disrespectful than the last. The enormity of the case pushed on his chest like the bullet was dropping through his body.

Billie and Baker had reduced the adoring couple from the photo to a few icy slabs of meat chilling in two metal coffins. Of course, Billie would go to any lengths to cover up. No judge in California would see what she did as anything but premeditated murder. They would see her hang for it.

And if Billie was seeking fame, she might just get it, though not in the way she was hoping.

Jimmy Evans went stone-pale, clapped his hands together, and muttered a prayer; for the departed couple, or perhaps for their safe escape from the waking nightmare. However, that seemed unlikely with not even so much as a window.

But James A. Anthony sat still, arms folded as he stared at the fridges. A hint of a tear glistened in the corner of his eye in the flashlight glow. The man seemed devastated. It seemed at odds that a man like James A. Anthony would give someone like Carl Bailey the time of day, but much like Billie's belief about life being messy had a ring of truth to it, people seemed no less complicated. From the frown lines that spilled from the corners of his nose like a puppet's mouth to his quivering lower lip, there was no denying the man had lost a dear friend.

"I'm sorry," said Rex. "I know you and Carl were close."

But the director didn't speak or move. He sat still, staring back at the chained refrigerators.

"Good Lord," Jimmy Evans whispered. "I still can't believe that sweet lady could be responsible for something so evil."

"People don't chain their fridges closed unless they have something to hide." Rex paused. "And I guess they don't lock men in their basement either."

Jimmy offered a titter, which seemed more out of pity than anything else.

"What about you, Mr. Horne?" asked Jimmy. "Are you okay? I mean, she shot you in the shoulder. That things gotta hurt."

As Rex swiveled to face the crooner, he shifted his shoulder a little too fast. The bullet scraped the bone. He winced, gripping his shoulder as he held his breath.

"Like someone's rammed a railroad spike into it," Rex grunted.

"Well, we need to get you out of here," Jimmy suggested.

Rex knew the man was well-intentioned, but he wanted to flatten the bible thumper for offering such a ridiculous suggestion. He bit the inside of his cheek and closed his eyes. Anthony didn't have as much self-restraint.

"You moron," he snapped. "How are we supposed to get to the hospital when we're locked in this god damned—"

"Don't use the Lord's name in vain!" Jimmy shouted.

"I'll use his name however I god damned want to, and another thing—"

The director's words faded into the background as Rex felt something hard and rectangular under his trenchcoat's chest pocket.

"Hey," he said.

The men carried on amongst themselves, arguing about everything from God to James A. Anthony's questionable start in the film industry. Rex tightened his mouth into a grimace as he waited for the men to realize he had solved their problem, but of course, they never did.

"Hey!" he screamed. The two men fell silent, staring at him. "I just had an idea. I think I know how to get us out of here."

Chapter 22

The men circled the fading flashlight as Rex detailed his plan. Their ragged hair and baggy eyes faded into the dying light. Jimmy Evans huddled, rocking like a man stranded on a desert island for three months instead of a basement for a couple days. And James A. Anthony had lost his spark, his already pale face drained of all color as he continued to look back at the refrigerators. It was the most pathetic regiment Rex had ever overseen. There was every chance someone was going to get shot. And with inflamed knees and a black and blue body, Rex seemed the most likely candidate.

But only a shoddy craftsman blamed his tools.

"This is ridiculous," said Anthony, who seemed distracted by his thoughts.

"I know," said Rex. "But what's your suggestion?"

"This whole scenario hinges on the fact that she will open the door. What if she doesn't?"

"She's gotta feed us," said Jimmy as the last flicker of a smile went out. "Doesn't she?"

"You saw how she was," said Anthony. "She doesn't want us to get out, but it doesn't seem like she has the gumption to kill us. Maybe if she ignores us long enough, we'll die of starvation. Two birds, one stone."

The director's words sunk into Rex's flesh like ice-cold claws. Rex imagined himself on the floor, intense burning in the pit of his stomach. Without the energy to lift his arm or call out for help, he would let out a dry gargle in the dark since the flashlight would fail long before them.

It could take more than a week to starve to death.

Rex fought the chill that tingled over his skin like an army of frozen ants. He cleared his throat and pushed on.

"We will get her to open the door," he said. "Because we are going to make as much noise as we can."

The men sat in silence, blank faces staring back at him.

"That's it," James A. Anthony scoffed. "That's your big plan. Make a lot of noise? Do you think we haven't screamed for help before? Nobody can hear us."

"Not nobody," said Rex. "Billie is on edge. The neighbors might not be able to hear us, but she's not going to want to take that chance. We play on her nerves enough, and she will open that door. She'll threaten you to keep quiet, and that's when we attack."

"There's enough space for me to hide in the shadows on the landing," Rex grabbed the flashlight and pointed at the wooden door, barely visible at the top of the stairs. The wooden landing sat about three feet wider than the doorway. "If I hide up there and wait for the perfect moment, I can take the gun from her. Without that, we can pin her to the ground and—"

Jimmy Evans stood, head shrunk into his shoulders as he paced. "But we aren't going to hurt her, surely."

"You think she gives a hoot whether you live or die here in this basement," James A. Anthony scoffed. "The woman was my friend, but I'm ready to plug her if it means getting out of this dump."

"Well, I guess you and I were just raised differently." Evans folded his arms. "I was raised in a good Christian household where I learned that *murder was a sin*."

"I'm not saying we *do* kill her, you bible-thumping ninny." James A. Anthony stood. "But if it comes to that, we need to do everything we can to survive."

The whole thing seemed so petty, like a Laurel and Hardy skit. It might've been funny if they weren't in a life and death situation, but their grating argument gnawed at his ears like a pair of sewer rats.

"Shut up, both of you!" Rex pounded his bruised fists on the concrete, but that only fuelled his anger. "We're all going to die of old age waiting for you two to get your act together. We're going ahead with this plan. She *will* come to the door, and I *will* grab her. I'll get the gun back, and when that happens, I need you two to pin her down for thirty seconds."

"What will you do?" asked Jimmy Evans.

Billie's footsteps tapped over by the door. She was in the kitchen.

"I don't have time to explain," Rex threw his arms up in the air and rose to his feet. "Thirty seconds, then after that, you run as fast as you can out the front door, and you keep running until there's no chance Billie has followed you. Understand?"

"You're not coming with us?" Evan's eyes widened.

"My running days are over, kid," Rex scoffed. "But I've got a plan, don't you worry about me. Just give me thirty seconds, and I'll take care of the rest."

An obnoxious honk rang through the basement like a crate of alarm clocks. Rex shielded his ears until the noise stopped, but Evans smiled like it was the second coming of Christ.

"It's the doorbell," said jimmy. "We're saved. We've gotta start making some noise right away."

It was far too late for a visitor. Rex could only imagine Virginia at the front door, demanding to speak to him, though he couldn't invent a reason. He threw his hands up like a mime trying to get their attention.

"Don't," he whispered.

"What do you mean, *don't?*" James A. Anthony's voice rumbled across the space.

"What if it isn't someone who can help us? What if it's an accomplice? Or worse yet, some innocent who came by? She has a gun up there, we alert them to our presence, and she might just put a bullet in the back of their skull."

Anthony's freckled face pinched into a withered sneer. "But—"

"We wait." Rex pointed a rigid finger at the man's ugly mug, then turned his back on the man as the footsteps thumped beyond the basement ceiling.

"And to what do I owe this dubious pleasure?" Billie's voice echoed through the ducts. "It's almost three in the morning."

Then came the unmistakably smug voice of Chaz Benson. "I received a phone call from Virginia Lancaster."

All Rex could do was smile. Thank God for Virginia and her penchant for worrying.

Benson continued his monologue as though he were some Dashiell Hammett character. "Seems her boyfriend, Rex Horne, said he was on a stakeout waiting for your husband to call. I thought that sounded a little odd since he said he would run any developments by me first."

Typical Benson. The clues practically punched him square in the jaw, but he was pouting like a four-year-old because he wasn't allowed to play with the big boys.

"A detective?" said Jimmy. "He might be able to hear us."

"Wait," Rex held up a hand.

"She told me that someone had attacked you *again*, and Rex Horne watched over you for the night. I needed to run some new information by him. Is he upstairs?"

"No," said Billie, a little too quickly. "He left. He discovered that my attacker was Betty Aldridge."

"Really?" said Benson, suspicion tinging his tone. "Because we found Betty Aldridge at the Hollywood Roosevelt, and the staff there said she hadn't left the hotel since she got there."

Rex clenched his jaw. *Come on, Benson. Figure it out.*

"Then, I don't know what to believe," Billie sobbed. "Just when I think this nightmare might be over, some new curveball comes to make things worse."

"Come now," said Benson. "I hate to see a pretty lady cry. We'll figure this out. What if Betty Aldridge had an accomplice? What if it's your husband?"

Billie sniffed. "You mean he was sharing her bed, too?"

"I'm afraid that might be the case," said Benson.

Rex rolled his eyes. Did he sound that pathetic to the other when Evans and Anthony eavesdropped on his heart to heart with the murderous lounge singer? Her guilt buzzed over her head like a neon sign, but Billie's delicate features had blinded Rex. He liked to think of himself as more sophisticated than the vice cop, but perhaps he was just another boy stupefied by a pretty little chippy.

Benson's comment left a pregnant pause in the conversation. Rex snapped out of his reverie as his escape window closed.

"Alright now," said Rex. "Make as much noise as you can."

Jimmy Evans screamed. Anthony knocked over an old filing cabinet, slamming the draws, while Rex shook the chained refrigerators, ignoring his bruised body and trying not to think about the fridge's contents.

"What was that?" Benson's voice barely carried over the clangs and screams.

"Keep going," Rex hollered.

"You know what it's like with big old places like this, their bones creak and moan, just like some old geezer."

Silence.

"I suppose you're right," Benson answered with a chuckle.

"Are you kidding me?" Rex groaned. "What kind of fatheaded cop hears a strange noise and doesn't investigate? That little bastard's incompetence is finally gonna kill me."

"Thank you for dropping by, detective," Billie's voice filtered through the ducts with a mechanical echo. "I do feel safer knowing you're here to watch over me."

"All part of the job," said Benson. "I'll be down at the Central Police Station. You can call me any time if anything happens."

There was a slam of the door.

"Well, that went well." Anthony scoffed.

"She's gonna be furious," Jimmy Evans chewed his nails.

"Furious enough to open the door," said Rex.

He slapped his barefoot on the first step, clutching his burning shoulder with his right hand and gripping the pinewood handrail with his left. The rail wobbled as the detective pressed his weight against it, pushing on the cracked wood as he heaved his body onto the next step as Billie pounded across the floor, muttering to herself.

Rex made it a few steps from the landing before he saw the silhouette of Billie's feet by the door. Rex froze. He didn't have enough time. If she swung the door open, he would need to brace himself to lunge at the woman.

"Probably thought you were clever with that little stunt," Billie's voice thundered from behind the door. "Well, I guess you leave me now a choice. I'm going to have to kill you."

A jangle of keys came from the other side. Rex's body relaxed. She still fumbled with the shoddy padlock. He climbed the last few steps and his in the darkness. James A. Anthony and Jimmy Evans stood at the bottom of the stairs. Neither seemed to share Rex's optimism for the plan, but so long as they kept their mouths shut and did as he said, he couldn't give a rat's ass.

Click.

The padlock thumped to the tiles, and the door creaked open. Rex pressed his battered back against the hard wall, forcing himself into the darkness as he waited for the gun-wielding singer to spot him before he could strike.

"I don't want to do this," Billie sniveled. "Despite what you think about me, I am not going to enjoy this."

Tears rolled down the woman's soft cheeks as she peered at the men downstairs. Rex had a maximum of a few seconds before she realized he was missing, so he lunged from the darkness and grabbed the gun with both hands. She fired as Rex pushed her arm up.

Crack.

Plaster dust floated down over their heads as they tumbled to the checker-tiled floor, and Rex couldn't help but see the face of Felix, the poor boy he killed back in Brittany. Rex pushed his guilt down as he slammed the singer's hand against the tiles until she let go. The gun flew from her hand and slid across the tiles.

"Get up here," Rex screamed down the corridor. "Hold her down. Thirty seconds, remember?"

James A. Anthony pinned the woman down, screaming at her for answers about why she killed his best friend. Jimmy Evans pinned the woman's other arm, slowly counting from one. Rex grabbed the gun and limped into the kitchen towards the reception dining hall.

Chapter 23

Rex clutched the chunky phone receiver to his ear, pacing the reception office at The Neptune Club, muttering under his breath as Evans and Anthony raced out of the lounge. The men stumbled over one another as they ran towards the front door. Anthony grabbed the gold handle and jiggled it with a series of violent cracks that sounded like the ornate metal was going to snap off.

"It isn't working," Evans screamed.

"Gee, why aren't you the detective?" Anthony groaned. "Now, get out of my way."

The director pushed Jimmy Evans away, grabbed the blue garbage can sitting by the door, and hurled the slightly rusted metal through the glass. The pane exploded in a sharp crack. Jimmy Evans barged past and stumbled into the streets, screaming for help. But James A. Anthony turned back, stared at Rex, and gave him a nod.

"Make sure she pays for what she did to Carl," he said.

Rex nodded with a grimace, and the man disappeared into the night.

"Why couldn't you just play along?"

Billie stood in the doorway. Rex froze as he reached for his gun, then looked down at the pistol between them. He hobbled over, but Billie was quicker, snatching the Colt and aiming it between his eyes from across the room. Her arms trembled as tears wobbled in her dark eyes.

"Why couldn't you just leave things alone?" Billie sniffed in the doorway. "I had everything under control."

"By murdering a couple of people and kidnapping a few more?"

The singer clutched the pistol so tight Rex felt it in *his* knuckles.

"You know, I thought you might add some credibility to the case and help cover my tracks, but like a bumbling fool, you've lost your gun for the second time." Her voice cracked as she shook her head. "I was paying for *Murder, My Sweet*, and instead, I got *The Ghost Breakers*."

"That was why you did this in the end?" asked Rex. "So Hollywood could turn it into a hundred thousand dollar farce?"

"You're not half as clever as you think you are, Horne," Billie scoffed. "You still think this is all about me and what I get out of it. I don't gain anything. I did this for good old-fashioned revenge."

"And that's when you killed him in Brentwood and brought them back in those refrigerators."

Billie staggered back, terror radiating from her eyes.

"How could you know that?" she whispered.

"But then the loose ends started to show," Rex charged on, still holding up his aching arms. "Will Baker's knowledge of what you did, then people started sniffing around and asking questions, so you had to stop everyone from prying into the truth. But you couldn't stop *me*."

Billie rested the gun flat against her forehead as she sobbed. Her nightgown swayed in the night wind. Like a wailing ghost, a lost soul tormented by her past life.

"Do you realize how humiliating it was?" she screamed. "To have my husband run away with the backstabbing slut who already stole my voice. I snapped. Isn't everyone allowed to have a moment of weakness?"

Billie's eyes inflated to the size of a cartoon character as she batted them at the detective. Rex wasn't sure if it was the crisp air whistling through the broken door pane or the bullet wound throbbing in his shoulder, but something had broken her spell on him.

"This was no impulse killing," said Rex. "You planned this. You had left crumbs about your husband's alleged abuse for me to find since the moment I met you. *Every* clue that came my way, including the flyer that Mr. Baker no doubt put in that locker, was carefully curated so I would do my job and pin the whole thing on Carl. You got to salvage your reputation after the embarrassing truth got out. You weren't just humiliated, but you were a victim. That way, nobody could say it was your fault."

Billie dropped her hands from her face. Tears leaked from her puffy eyes.

"Good for you," the singer snapped. "You figured it out. Does that make you feel like a big man now? Sending me to prison? I loved Carl, really, and it pained me to do what I did, but that bitch had what was coming to her. She thought she could steal a part of me just because she couldn't sing. That's not my fault. I told you, you need a soul to sing."

"I don't think that's exactly true," said Rex as he dipped into his pocket.

"Keep your hands where I can see them!" Billie screamed.

"I'm just reaching for this."

Rex pulled the blood-splattered card from his pocket and flicked it across the floor. It sailed through the air like a spitfire, landing perfectly at the woman's feet.

"What is it?" Billie's voice quivered.

"You see, Billie," Rex kept his voice low, trying to quell the fire in her callous comments about Miss Lake. "You didn't have to use any *soul*. You just sang for me. like a canary."

Sweat beaded on the singer's face. Rex took a step closer.

"You're not the only one that can pull some strings. I called Benson while you were dealing with the other two. He's listening right now, and he's probably sent a whole fleet of cops over here. I sympathize with what your husband put you through, but if you think for one second I'm going to stand by your cavalier attitude towards his murder, not to mention Miss lake, then you don't know me as well as you think you do."

Billie's face tightened as her eyes darted from Rex to the telephone.

"You're bluffing."

"You can speak to him if you like," Rex shrugged.

Billie grabbed the Colt and wedged it under her jawline, squeezing the trigger. There was a click. Then she tried again. And again. Rex's smug energy drained from his body as he now saw a hollow woman with nothing left. Billie was a rollercoaster. Just when he was ready to write her off, she did something that made her seem human again.

"I took the bullets out," Rex sighed, stepping closer. "I'm sorry, and for what it's worth, *I* don't get any pleasure out of this either."

"I helped Caroline out, offered my voice for the film." Billie wept. "I didn't even ask for my share of the money, but just the recognition. Do you realize what it's like to work hard on something, put your entire heart and soul into it, only to have some white woman come and claim it as her own?"

Rex's chest sunk. While her actions were deplorable, he could understand why she would do what she did. Caroline Lake was nothing more than the Chaz Benson of her story.

"Caroline shouldn't have done that to you," Rex softened his voice.

"You think it ends with her?" Billie scoffed. "This happens every day. Colored folks everywhere have their work stolen because whites think their time and effort is worth more than ours. And as if that wasn't bad enough, she took my husband from me too.

"I stood by that man, worked day and night to keep this place together, and sang songs I couldn't stand, so the white folks kept paying the bills. And how did he thank me after years of dedication? He steps out on me with that pasty-white hussy."

Despite everything she had done, the detective sincerely wished for the singer to find solace, just as much as he hoped he could find it himself. Billie collapsed to the ground and dropped the pistol, which rattled to the floor.

"I'm truly sorry," said Rex. "If I had known—"

Rex wasn't sure how to finish that sentence.

"What difference does it make?" her usually melodious voice fell flat. "My life is over now. I'm going to lose this club. It's the only thing I have."

Rex didn't say another word. He stumbled onto his backside and sat beside the woman as she wept, wiping her eyes with her gossamer nightgown. He placed a hand over Billie's.

"I'll wait with you," said Rex. "I'll speak with Benson when he gets here. Maybe we can work something out."

She may have been guilty of murder, that was her choice alone, but if he were in the singer's situation, would he be so cool, calm, and willing to change? Hell, his entire argument with Virginia revolved around his stubbornness with Benson.

Red lights flashed across Sunset Boulevard.

Benson charged in, pistol at the ready. He aimed the weapon at Billie's chest and screamed, "Get up. Now, on your feet!"

Billie did as the vice cop ordered, hands behind her head.

"Benson," said Rex as he clutched the wall and hauled onto his feet.

"Don't move, or I will shoot."

"Nobody's going to shoot anybody," said Rex.

"Tell me why I shouldn't plug you right now and be done with this."

"Private!" Rex roared. "Drop your weapon right now and listen to me, you sniveling little prick."

Benson glared at Rex with such palpable anger the detective was almost sure the vice cop would open fire on him, but he dropped his gun to the floor.

"Mrs. Bailey is surrendering of her own volition," Rex kept his hands in the air, limping towards Benson. "She isn't going to show any aggression, and you aren't going to shoot her. She's going to spend a long time making up for what she did, and you're going to give her that chance, you hear me?"

Two beat cops came in behind him, guns at the ready. Benson offered a wave of his hand, and they relaxed, holstering their pistols.

"Arrest this woman for the murder of Caroline Lake, Carl Bailey, and William Baker," Benson's eyes flicked to Rex. "And call an ambulance for Mr. Horne. He looks like he's on death's door."

Chapter 24

Rex lay in his hospital bed for the second time while Virginia sat opposite him in her green pinup dress, her hair styled under a matching hat. She sat on the tightly folded corner of the bed, swinging her crossed leg as she shot him a cherry-red smirk.

"You know, we must stop meeting like this, Mr. Horne," she said, her husky British accent like sweet music. "People will talk."

"We don't want Polly Whittingham blabbing about this one."

Rex chuckled, then took a sharp breath as a dull ache spread over his body, like laying paralyzed in the ring with a million microscopic Tony Zales, swinging hooks and jabs into his tender flesh.

"Oh my poor darling," Virginia pouted her lips. "I'm sure Polly Whittingham would love to hear the story of how you stopped that dastardly lounge singer from committing the perfect crime."

"Well, she's not going to hear it from me," Rex groaned.

Virginia seemed to pause, then she dropped her eyes to her red fingernails, brushing a finger over them as though she were dusting it. Despite her guilt, Rex couldn't muster the energy to care if she told the story to Polly Whittingham. It all seemed so trivial in light of everything that had happened the night before.

"What did you do?" Rex rolled his eyes with a smirk.

"I've been speaking with Benson."

"Why would you do that?" Rex shuffled upright with a moan.

Virginia tossed her hands on her hips as she seemed to brace herself for battle.

"Because I told him everything you should have back in France," the actress' tone galvanized. "I told him everything about Brittany and Holloway. He's outside now, and he wants to talk to you."

Virginia stared at him for a moment. Her stance looked ready for another bout, but her eyes seemed to sparkle with concern, as though she was worried she might push him away. Rex smiled, beckoning her over with one finger. About all he could manage without groaning in pain. She sidled up beside him.

"You're right," said Rex. "I've been a stubborn old fool. And besides, it might be nice to tell that little bastard how I really feel."

Virginia laughed, then leaned over and kissed him on the forehead. Rex smiled back. The tingle of her warm kiss felt good against his bruised skin.

"Now, I don't want to force you to do anything," said Virginia, "especially after everything you've been through, but if you just talk to the man, I'm sure—"

"Virginia," Rex chuckled. "You've been trying to convince me to talk to Benson from the beginning. Don't back out on me now that I'm finally going to do it. I might start to think you actually *enjoy* fighting with me."

"How could I not enjoy our little repartee?" Virginia winked, then shouted over her shoulder. "You can come in now, Detective Benson."

Benson walked into the room in a grey coat, his matching hat in his hands. He offered Rex a smile, but Rex didn't return it. He might have turned a leaf with Virginia, but Benson had a long road to redemption ahead of him.

"Hey, Major," he said, without the usual vibrato. "How are you feeling?"

"Like I was shot and thrown down a flight of stairs," Rex groaned.

"Why don't I give you both a moment," said Virginia and slunk out into the hall.

Silence hung over the room as Benson shuffled closer, like a dog that knew it was in for a beating. He made it to Rex's bedside, and his face dropped into a frown.

"I'm sorry," said Benson. "I should've known something was going on. I should've checked out that noise. If only I'd—"

"Forget about it," Rex cut him off. "It all worked out at the end. How is Billie?"

"Alive and well." Benson folded his arms. "Enjoying her stay at the California Institution for Women in Chino. Still better than I think she deserved, better than Caroline Lake got."

"Maybe." Rex shrugged. "But don't you think we owe it to her to have the chance to make up for everything she did."

Benson paused and brushed his fingers over his hat.

"Do you think you could forgive me? Virginia told me everything that happened. I didn't know Holloway's death was my fault. I never even knew you were mad at me."

Rex said nothing, not because he was pouting but because what else was he meant to say? He spent so long hating Benson for everything he did. Now it seemed hard to shake the habit. But if he didn't, was he any better than Benson was towards Billie?

"Come on, Sir." He smiled at the man. "Work with me, help me out with vice? I need someone like you to whip my butt when you need to. Keep me honest. Surely there's something I can do for you. Anything."

"Well," Rex paused. "There is one thing."

Chapter 25

Rex sat in the empty outdoor dining area outside La Sirena on West 5th Street in Santa Ana. A quaint single-story Spanish-style building with terracotta tiled roof and walls rendered in pale yellow. The little Mom and Pop Mexican restaurant shrunk between the two-story buildings that lined the street, wedged between a Carl's Jr. and a Coach clothing store.

A grizzled man in a greased stained shirt walked a plate over to Rex's table with a smile, although the dark circles around his eyes indicated a lack of sleep. Rex had some theories about why. The man placed the plate of something called Huevos Rancheros in front of him and stared at him with an expectant grin. Rex grabbed a forkful of shredded meat, beans, and avocado. He put them in his mouth, expecting something so violent it might make him wretch. Instead, the juicy beef melted on his tongue, offering a little kick. Rex's eyes widened as he turned to the man with a smile.

"This is delicious," said Rex.

"It should be," said the man. "My Abuela taught me to make it back in Veracruz. That lady sure knew how to cook."

Rex set down his fork. Where could he even start? How could he tell the man what he drove thirty-three miles to say to him?

"You're Miguel Martinez?" Rex dry swallowed.

"Ay Dios mío," the man muttered under his breath, sitting down. "This is about Manuel, isn't it?"

Rex nodded. "Why don't you sit down?"

"Are you with the police?"

"No." Rex sucked his teeth as he tried to find the words.

The detective placed the crinkled hundred-dollar bill on the table and flattened it. "Manuel gave me this because he wanted me to find you."

"Where is he?" Miguel beamed with a crooked grin that stabbed into Rex's chest like a knife. "I haven't seen my kid brother in so long."

Rex couldn't bring himself to say the words. Like a chicken, he stared down at his food, mentally slapping himself across the face and telling himself to man up and tell the cook his brother was dead; he deserved to know the truth. Miguel's face crumpled in on itself as the cook buried his face in his hands, running them through his cropped black hair. He wept.

"I'm sorry," Rex's voice came out in a whisper.

"I was so stupid," he groaned into his hands. "All this over nothing because he owed me a few dollars. And now we'll never get that time back."

Rex put his hand over the hundred-dollar bill and pushed Benjamin Franklin's chubby face towards the scruffy cook.

"I want you to have this," he said.

"No." Miguel shook his head, pushing the banknote back. "I couldn't accept this."

"Please," said Rex, sliding the bill across the table. "Your brother wanted to see you, and I couldn't make that happen. I don't deserve this money, but this way, maybe he can finally pay you back."

Rex grabbed his fork and took another bite of his Huevos Rancheros, and listened to an afternoon of stories about a man he barely knew. He wasn't just some corpse in a Skid Row back alley. He was a talented painter and wanted to travel through Europe, go to art galleries, and create his own art. As time passed, Miguel laughed, reminiscing about his brother's life rather than dwelling on his death.

"I'm sorry, I've been talking about myself for the last couple of hours," asked Miguel. "What about you? What's your story?"

"Don't worry about me," Rex scoffed with a wave of his hand. "I'm just happy listening."

Get a Free Book!

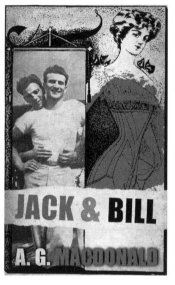

**GET A FREE
HOLLYWOODLAND
MYSTERY NOVELLA**
Jack and Bill is a fast-paced mystery novella, which you can get free if you sign up to A. G. Macdonald's mailing list. The story is set a month before *Silent Siren* and follows Rex as he is pulled back into the Hollywood scene by a couple of familiar faces. They are being blackmailed and need Rex's help to solve the case before their careers are destroyed.

In addition to this book, the mailing list also has a monthly newsletter with exclusive news and information, as well as recommendations for classic movies that inspired each book.

Find details at www.agmacdonaldauthor.com

Also from A. G. Macdonald

Hollywood: February 1946

Ingénue actress, Cinderella, is found dead in her bathtub. The case seems like another actress overdose until the young starlet's stepmother walks into the office of Rex Horne: a two-time war vet turned private detective. She tells him that the young actress was receiving threats from a fan. Was Cinderella's death an accident, or the result of a jealous stalker?

About Author

A. G. Macdonald is a geek that loves all things film (both modern and classic). His debut novel, *Cinderella: Dead at 25!* and sequel *Silent Siren* were inspired by his love of classic Hollywood films like *Sunset Boulevard, Casablanca,* and The *Thin Man.*

Acknowledgments

2022 has been an insane year. It's still a little crazy that I've already released a *second* novel and have almost finished writing a third (after many years of trying to *perfect* my first novel, which may never see the light of day). But these things don't happen in a vacuum. Many people have helped, both directly and indirectly, to bring Rex Horne and this cast of characters to life.

One of my biggest inspirations is my dear friend Amy. Though we have never met in person, you have no idea what our friendship means to me personally or how impactful our discussions about everything from manga to *Twin Peaks* have been. Each of these conversations, not to mention your endless support and being my self-appointed 'cheerleader' has motivated me to believe that this is possible to complete these projects and that people may want to *read this stuff*.

You will never know just how much it means to me.

Then there is R. K. Gold, one of my oldest friends on the internet and my number one source for conversations on all things author-based. I have loved every minute of our chats about creativity (not to mention our watch-throughs for Ghibli movies and *The Boondocks*.)

Then there are my real-world family and friends. While there is another book's worth of real-life people I could thank, but know that the constant support of my family and friends has formed the basis of everything I do and given me the confidence I needed to type the first words on the keyboard. None of this would have happened without you, but hands off my royalties! (Just kidding, I swear).

And then there is Montgomery, who *really* earned her money on this one. While the writing process came easier this time around, and I believe that this second installment is infinitely better than the first, this was the one I found most difficult to straddle the line between representing the 1940s in a believable light without endorsing some of its more questionable beliefs. Montgomery did a phenomenal job of critiquing my more complicated characters so that they also struck the right tone.

I am so lucky to have an editor who rocks!

Lastly, I need to thank you, the reader, for returning to Hollywoodland with me. I cannot say this with enough sincerity that it does not escape me that you have taken a chance on these stories. I am very aware that the markets are becoming more flooded with every passing day, and you could've chosen somebody else, but you didn't. And for that, I will be forever grateful.

Please consider leaving a review on Amazon and Goodreads if you enjoyed this novel. These reviews are instrumental to my success as an author. If you loved the Old Hollywood storytelling, you might consider signing up to my mailing list to receive updates, recommendations, and a free Hollywoodland mystery novella if you haven't already. Thanks to all those people who have already signed up. I can't wait to chat with you there.

Sincerely,

A. G. Macdonald.

Coming May 2022

May 1946

Rex Horne is trying to get his life on track, and joins Alcoholics Anonymous. But just as he feels he is getting a grasp on his life, Detective Benson drags him into a case involving an unidentified girl found strangled and left for dead in Grand Park.

The investigation leads Rex to the Magic Mirror Circus, which just arrived in town. But the big top holds a secret to Rex's past that he would rather keep buried.

Printed in Great Britain
by Amazon

78951200R00124